Angela Moore

Conversion of a Pimp:

Joanna II

Angela Moore

Disclaimer:

This is a work of fiction. Names, characters, businesses, places, events and incidents are either the products of the author's imagination or used in a fictitious manner. Any resemblance to actual persons, living or dead, or actual events is purely coincidental.

Angela Moore

Acknowledgments

Because a percentage of all book sales in the Conversion of a Pimp book series, up to $100,000.00, go towards a college fund for my little cousin Taelor Alexander, I'd like to say THANK YOU!

Conversion of a Pimp: Joanna II

~Matthew 11:28-30~

28 *"Come to Me, all you who are weary and burdened, and I will give you rest.*

29 *Take My yoke upon you and learn from Me, for I am gentle and humble in heart, and you will find rest for your souls.*

30 *For My yoke is easy and My burden is light."*

Table of Contents

Chapter One
~Rufus~

The Point of No Return

I sat on my dorm bed in a panic, shaking like I had on a bikini in Alaska. My mind couldn't process what I'd just read. *How can Rufus be here! How in the hell can he be here!* I threw my phone onto my bed wondering how such a perfect weekend could end so messed up. With tears streaming down my face, I put my head between my legs and that's when the scent of my urine assaulted my nose. With the quickness I snapped out of my moment of despair and went into *zoom-zoom* mode.

I knew my roommate would be back soon so I jumped up and sprang into action. I got fresh clothes, yanked up my soiled bedding and threw them onto the floor. I changed my bed linen then ran down the hall to the dorm shower.

I hurriedly got undressed and as before, because of Rufus, I was once again letting my tears go down the drain as I showered. I was having another good cry, compliments of that no good for nothing devil! I stood under the water dazed as I talked to the Lord begging and pleading with Him to get me out of this situation. It hadn't been thirty minutes since I'd read that text and already I felt so entrapped and in bondage. I didn't know what to do. I felt like a caged animal. *Why was Rufus doing this to me! Why can't he just leave me alone and go on with his life?* I couldn't comprehend why he was even there. This is a freaking Christian college! Rufus didn't know nor did he care about Christ or anything He had to offer, so why in the heck was he there!?

Although I had the shower steaming hot, I was still shaking like a leaf. I knew I couldn't be in there for long so I got my emotions under control, washed up as fast as I could and got dressed. After that, I took my pissy clothes and bedding to the laundry, hoping to wash away my anxiety. Once I'd started the washer, I leaned up against it and started biting on my nails, trying to come up with a solution to my problem. There was no way I could stay on the campus with Rufus walking on it, absolutely no way. But what could I do? I couldn't go back home. If I attempted that, it would be such a huge red flag to my parents that they would drill me like a drill Sargent trying to figure out why I had abruptly left school. And even if I came up with a lame excuse they would pray to The Lord for the real answer and

He very rarely refused my parents anything they requested. There was no way my folks could find out about Rufus, ever.

I thought about my brothers but knew I couldn't tell them either. They were way too over protective to risk getting Rufus hurt. I didn't want anything to happen to Rufus; I just wanted him out of my fucking life.

While thinking of a master plan I remembered that I hadn't wiped my piss up off the floor so I sprinted up to my room, grabbed some Clorox wipes, and then went to work. Just as I was spraying some smell goods throughout the room Faith walked in. *Whew! That was close.*

****

I was on high alert during the remainder of the semester. I was scared to go anywhere for fear that I would run into Rufus.

There had been plenty of times when Faith and some of my other friends would ask me to hang with them and I would flat out refuse. I was on edge most of the time so I wasn't taking any chances. That devil being in such close proximity of me caused me to damn near have a panic attack and it seemed that no matter how hard I prayed, that monkey wouldn't jump off my back.

Although Timothy still wasn't my type, we had become very close friends since starting school. Initially, if I was walking across campus and he saw me, he'd catch up and walk me to my dorm room or we'd go to the library to study together, but after Rufus sent me that text, I shut all that down, too. Anytime I heard a male calling my name it made me jump because I'd think it was Rufus. So, one afternoon when Timothy had yelled for me to slow my roll, I did just the opposite and started doing a sprint walk to my dorm. That boy was not to be deterred and started a slow jog in my direction which allowed him to catch up with me in no time. Once by my side he grabbed me by my arm and spun me around. When I looked into my friends concerned eyes, I dropped my head, my books, and purse and then burst out in tears.

I had been running for months and couldn't run anymore. Walking around with my anxiety on my shoulder had been such a heavy weight I couldn't carry it any longer. As Timothy laid his book bag down, he simultaneously pulled me into his arms and started rocking me back and forth. I wrapped my arms around my friend and with my face in the crook of his neck, cried like a newborn baby. I squeezed and held on to Timothy so tight that I thought I felt him grimace but he didn't let me go. I couldn't help it, my brain felt like it was being smushed as the words "I'm here" danced around in my damn head. *Why is he here? Why in the hell is he here!?* As I emptied my anguish into my friend's neck, I didn't care who saw me crying. I couldn't take it anymore, I just couldn't.

Once I got myself under control, Timothy took a step back and placed both his hands on my shoulders. He then took a handkerchief out of his pocket and helped me wipe some of my tears away. He pulled me back into his embrace and asked "Do I need to call your brothers?" I took a big step backwards, and while hiccupping, I started shaking my head back and forth so hard, my neck started hurting. Timothy put a crooked smile on his face and said "Look Joanna, you had best believe you have all kinds of angels here on this campus watching over you. Do you really think that God would send you here without any? We don't serve a God like that. He knows what's going on with you more than any of us ever will. Hasn't He been good to you thus far?" While blowing my nose in his handkerchief, I shook my head up and down. He then asked "Did you read the verse of the day that I sent you?" That question caused me to look like a deer in headlights.

Rufus had me so off my mental game, that I hadn't been truly focused on the spiritual, only gripped by fear. Coming to that realization caused me to break down again. Timothy pulled me back into his arms and quietly spoke "Its ok, Joanna. It's ok. We all lose focus at times. It's just that when The Lord has allowed us to realize where we've fallen short, we address it, dust ourselves off, and then get back on track. Now, the verse of the day was from 2nd Timothy Ch. 1:7 'For God hath not given us the spirit of fear; but of power, and of love, and of a sound mind.' Hold on to that Joanna.

14

Embrace the power He has given you and stop giving the devil the victory. I've watched you pull away from me and everybody else for the last few months. As friends, I didn't want to pry, but as your brother in Christ, I am your keeper and could not continue to watch you suffer. We can conquer this together Joanna, and besides, two are better than one."

I wanted so badly to believe Timothy, I really did, but that Rufus was as evil as evil could get.

As my friend held me, my mind did a quick review of the hell Rufus had put me through, and then I stopped myself and kept it real. My mind did a quick review of the things *I had allowed* Rufus to put me through. My current situation wasn't all Rufus's fault; I had chosen to listen to the voice of another, and at that very moment I was suffering the consequences because of it.

I started saying the verse of the day in my head *2nd Timothy Ch. 1:7 For God hath not given us the spirit of fear; but of power, and of love, and of a sound mind. 2nd Timothy Ch. 1:7 For God hath not given us the spirit of fear; but of power, and of love, and of a sound mind. 2nd Timothy Ch. 1:7 For God hath not given us the spirit of fear; but of power, and of love, and of a sound mind.*

I said it over and over again until I made it my own. It was like Timothy knew I was having a battle within my mind. I was dealing with my fear, so he stood there patiently, without saying a word, waiting on me to finish. When he saw the strain slowly leave my face, he put another crooked smile on his, and then whispered "Now see, that's the Joanna I know".

He picked up all my crap, and then his book bag, and placed it over his shoulder. He put his arm around my waist, pulled me close, and softly kissed me on my forehead. He stepped back and then gently spoke "It's time to start living again little lady, ok?"

I put a small smile on my face, and in a soft voice answered "Ok".

As we started walking towards my dorm Timothy threw his arm around my shoulder. I was starting to feel a semblance of peace again and with each and every step I took; I left a piece of my burden behind me, hoping for a better future. And who knows, maybe Rufus had sent me that text and was lying. Maybe he wasn't really here. Besides, I hadn't seen nor heard from him since the day he'd sent me that text, and that too, gave me a glimmer of hope.

Timothy walked me to my dorm door, opened it for me, handed me all my stuff then said "No more of this moping around young lady, ya hear. We're way too young to be stressed out about stuff that's in the hands of the Lord, and besides all that, you know those angels I mentioned earlier?" I shook my head up and down then replied "Yes, Timothy. I know The Lord has His angels watching over me" and then gave a little chuckle.

Timothy stood boldly, lifted my chin with his index finger, looked me directly into my eyes, and remarked "Oh yeah, that's for sure. But it's those dark angels that nigga Rufus needs to be worried about, because those angels were sent by your big brother Jonathan, and they are all over this campus, looking for that nigga". He removed his finger, kissed me softly on my forehead, and then walked away.

I guess it took a minute for what Timothy had said to register, because as soon as I took the first step to enter my dorm, I stopped, quickly turned around, and watched as Timothy, in a mellow casual stride, made his way to his own dorm room. I immediately thought *what in the world is Timothy talking about dark angels? And how in the hell does he know about Rufus?*

****

Because it was such a nice day, I retracted my steps, and decided to sit on a bench that was under an old oak tree that was across from my dorm. I concluded that it probably wasn't a good idea for me to be in my dorm room alone, especially with the emotional state I was in. I also felt a little one on one time with The Lord while basking in His beautiful weather was just what the doctor ordered.

As I stuffed Timothy's handkerchief in my pocket, I began to let the words he'd spoken about Rufus marinate in my mind, but soon shut my brain down and dismissed those thoughts. Instead, I held on to my friends words of hope, and since The Lord had used him to give me a little peace, I refused to let the devil steal it away with thoughts of Rufus.

I put my ear plugs in my ears, then pressed play on my iPod and listened to some good ole a cappella singing while flipping through some of my biblical studies notes. I was starting to feel real good about life when the burden of the things I'd been going through lifted. So as I scanned my papers and listened to uplifting songs, I thanked God over and over again for the gift of friendship I had in Timothy.

I was in "Praise zone" when I felt a light tap on my shoulder that dang near scared me to death. With both hands on my chest I stood up to see who had rudely messed up my flow. I turned around and I saw Faith with her hands in the same position as mine, but instead of being buck eyed with fear, she was bent over in laughter. She was laughing so hard it caused me to put a smile on my face. When she could catch her breath she sang "Giiiiirl! I wish you coulda seen yo face" then howled in laughter again. When she said that, I too started laughing. There wasn't no shame in my making fun of myself. Shoot, that laugh was well overdue, so I basked in it.

After the both of us calmed down Faith asked "Girl what has been going on with you? You been dodging me like I gotta disease or something. Oh shoot! Before I forget, did you get that package I laid on your bed? It came at about 2 o'clock today". I asked "What package?" and as Faith spoke, I didn't get just plain ole "Excited." Heck naw! That's too simple of a word. I got "Super-duper excited," because every now and then my big brothers would send me "Just because" gifts, and they spared no coins when it came to making me happy.

****

The last fantastic present I had received came from Jude. He'd sent me a gift certificate for a year of free body massages at one of the upscale massage parlors in the city. But the significance of his gift was that he had purchased two, one for me and one for Faith. Jude making that move placed him in my "Favorite big brother spot," because everybody knew that he was super frugal when it came to his coins. Jude purchasing two gift certificates was a huge sacrifice for him because he never spent a dime unless it was on a new suite for church, or for a fellowship meal someone in the congregation was hosting, so the massage gifts were dang near like experiencing a miracle.

The very fact that Jude was a penny pincher showed in the first gift he had given me while at college, a 5$ McDonald's gift card. When I opened that little envelope and saw the amount, I put my hand on my hip, looked up at Jude and asked "Ummm, sooo, what am I supposed to buy with this, a kids meal?" The crazy thing is he had the nerve to look at me like "You so ungrateful." *What?! Ungrateful? Whatever!* I put that gift card in my purse and that's where it stayed.

Now Jonathan was a different story. From day one he laced me with good gifts, with the first one being a small dainty Ann Cline watch I'd seen at the mall. Just about every gift I received from him was something I had admired from afar, but couldn't afford. What puzzled me was how he knew about the things I wanted. I would later find out that whenever he was about to purchase me something, he'd call mommy and ask her to pick my brain to find out what my hearts desires were, and that's how he'd hit the nail on the head almost every time.

I guess Jude got tired of me oohing and ahhing over Jonathan's gifts, because the next thing I knew, Jude had stepped up his gift game, and I became a blessed little lady because of it.

The competition between the two was getting fierce, and I had really doubted if Jude would be able to hang with Jonathan and his never empty wallets, but thus far he'd proven me and everybody else wrong. But then the rubber was about to meet the road because after Jude had sent me those gift certificates, Jonathan sent me the fire red cowgirl boots that I had been silently stalking on the web. That there move made Jude's massages look like that 5$ McDonalds gift card he'd given me. Getting me those boots placed Jonathan into the "fat big brother brownie points" slot, because those mugs were over 700$. That price bracket was the most spent on me thus far, so I assumed Jude had sent me something that would, in the blink of an eye, trump Jonathan's gift. They'd played the "I love you more than he

20

does" game since the day they'd dropped me off at school and I must say, I was oh so very happy to be the recipient of my big brothers sibling rivalry.

****

Because I knew that Jude wouldn't allow Jonathan to reign on the "Favorite big brother" throne for long, I hopped my little happy butt up off that bench, and then made a mad dash to my room. I could not wait to open the gift that would temporarily place him in the "You will forever be my favorite brother" spot. I ran into my room and saw a little white envelope in the center of my bed. In my mind I thought *I sure hope he ain't going back to his old ways* as I picked it up and flopped myself onto my bed. I opened the envelope and saw a 5,000$ Gift card for Louis Vuitton inside. *Aww shoot! Jude dun really stepped up his dang on game!!!* I could barely wait to see how Jonathan was going to beat that.

When I pulled out the card a small thin slip of paper floated out as well and landed on the floor. I stared at that gift card for a good ten minutes, reading the small print, and then put it in my nightstand for safe keeping. I reached down and picked up the piece of paper that had fallen and noticed that it was light as a feather, almost like tissue paper. I lay back down and flipped the piece of paper over. When I read what was typed on there

I wanted to faint. In pretty italic print it said "Hey Juicy".

I sat straight up in the bed and read and reread those pretty little words again and again, and then tore the paper up. I ran to the bathroom and flushed those shreds down the toilet, and at the same time thought *if only I hadn't memorized his number at the rink before flushing IT down the toilet.*

I walked back to my bed, hit my knees to the floor and prayed like I was Jesus in the garden of Gethsemane.

While praying I heard Faith bounce into the room and ask "Girl, what one of yo fine brothers send you this time?" but stopped short when she saw me on my knees. I pleaded with the Lord to help me deal with the situation I felt I had no control over. I begged him to remove Rufus from my life and asked Him to give me the faith I needed to stand strong if He decided not to. I was praying so hard I felt sweat rolling down my back and under my armpits. I calmed down and repeated one of my favorite bible verses, Philippians 4:6-7 'Be anxious for nothing; but in everything by prayer and supplication with thanksgiving let your requests be made known to God. And the peace of God, which surpasses all comprehension, will guard your hearts and your minds in Christ Jesus.' I said that verse over and over again, until I obtained the peace that was promised.

When I had finished Faith apologized then asked her question again. I opened my nightstand drawer and pulled out the gift card. I put it in my purse, stood up and headed for the door. With my hand on the knob, I turned and looked into Faith's jovial face and said "Girl, nothing to write home about" then walked out the door.

****

I went back to the bench and sat under that old oak tree for about five minutes. I'd come to the conclusion that I was tired of the whole Rufus fiasco, and that I wasn't going to run from my problems anymore and that it was time for me to face them head on, so I pulled out my cell phone and called Rufus. He answered on half a ring, like he'd been expecting my call. Before he could say a word I said "Leave me alone Rufus, why won't you just leave me alone? I don't want anything you have to offer. No gifts, no calls, no nothing, just leave me alone!" I was about to hang up when he said "Juicy, I ain't going no damn where so you might as well get used to it, and tell that punk ass Timothy that if I see his ass putting his arms around yo waist again, ima fuck his ass up! And by the way, you look real pretty in that purple" and then he hung up the phone.

With my phone still glued to my ear I stood up so fast my head hurt. I started turning around in a circle looking for Rufus. If I had any doubt that he was on campus, those doubts were quickly removed, because the purple shirt I was wearing proved otherwise.

I continued to turn in circles, then at the top of my lungs yelled "Leave me the hell alone" to absolutely nobody, and then hung up my phone. For some reason I felt empowered, like I wasn't scared of running into Rufus anymore, or afraid of anticipating his calls, or in the future, of getting more gifts from him and then discarding them like trash. I'd just resigned myself to not care anymore. I guess I had really reached my limit, and I was actually ok with that.

From that day forward I put my big girl panties on and lived my life as if Rufus was a non-factor and when we did eventually come into contact with each other, it was no big deal because I was over the bad boy per sauna that Rufus had exhibited.

My Word told me that my God was bigger than a thousand Rufus's, so that's what I stood on, and started living my life accordingly.

Chapter Two

~Rufus~

I'm the shadow man...

It was a brand new semester and I was hyped! I had made the dean's list, again, and was so happy to be on the right track, that when I saw Rufus's name on the dean's list too, I shrugged a shoulder and kept it movin'. I hadn't seen nor talked to Rufus since the gift card incident but knew that the school campus was way too small to keep us apart for long. And since I knew he was officially enrolled in classes, I also knew us bumping into each other was bound to happen; it was just a matter of when.

Although I didn't have too, I continued to over schedule my lessons. I wanted to continue with the rigorous schedule so that I wouldn't give the devil an opportunity to slither his way into any cracks in my life via fear, doubt, anxiety or any other mechanism. I was walking hand in hand with Christ and loving every minute of it. I thanked The Lord for both Timothy and Faith because they were both contributing to my spiritual growth and dependence on Christ, which was needed more than the air that I breathe. And although Rufus had thrown Timothy's name out there during our phone conversation, I threw that threat over my shoulder as well, concluding that Rufus's words had no power over me or my friends. But I would soon learn that when it came to Rufus, he never made idle threats, and everyone had best believe he was a boy of his word.

****

Although my schedule was tighter than the board of health, I made sure I had time to participate in one of my favorite activities, singing. It was a serious passion of mine and although my voice wasn't as beautiful as Jonathan's, I could still hold my own. When I saw a flyer that said the school was having auditions for the school chorus, I took my chances and auditioned. In the past I had listened to the schools chorus CDs religiously. My parents purchased them on a consistent basis because they believed in supporting Christian education. They also made regular donations by sponsoring a student or two who had a desire to teach the gospel, but lacked the funds to accomplish their goal. I surmised that if I was able to be a part of a ministry that was dear to my parent's heart, I would make my dear old folks very proud.

My audition was a piece of cake and although my family was known throughout the brotherhood, my

26

prayer was that if I made the cut, it would be because of my gifts and not because of my family name. I loved singing and would be honored to be a part of this great opportunity, but I also saw the chorus as an extracurricular activity, not a necessity. I understood that I was there for an education but knew that if I made the list, I'd put just as much effort into the singing group as I did to my studies, so I was good. The day had arrived and once again, I would be calling home with good news, and to be honest, my name being on the list had really shocked the heck outta me.

Because I'd grown up listening to the songs that the school had produced, I knew their singing group was top notch. I wasn't knocking my abilities, I was just aware of the material they birth and wanted to make sure I made The Lord and the school proud. When I told my parents that I'd made the chorus, they were extremely happy and so were Jonathan and Jude. All I wanted to do was cause a smile to be placed on my families face, and since I'd become refocused and gotten back on track, going backwards wasn't an option.

It was during the first day of chorus rehearsal that I ran into Rufus. His was the first face I saw when I walked into the auditorium and the reason I'd immediately noticed him was because of the wheelchair he was sitting in. I boldly walked right past him and as I did, I noticed that he had a broken leg and black eye. I couldn't help but think *I'm sure he had it coming to him,* but then I stopped myself.

Yes, Rufus had been more than extra towards me, but that wasn't cause for him getting hurt. I felt bad for thinking that he reaped what he'd sown, so I said a little prayer for him then ran into the arms of my good friend Timothy.

Since my snot session, I hadn't been in the presence of Timothy often, but we text daily. He was a true friend and helped me in my healing process while never allowing me to waiver or make excuses for my shortcomings. He held me accountable to my bible reading and reinforced it by continuing to send me his verses of the day. As I jumped into his arms, I could feel daggers being placed into my back as the temperature rose 50 degrees because of Rufus's seething anger. I didn't even care, and as Timothy put me down, I followed his eyes as they met Rufus's. I grabbed his arm and led him to the opposite side of the stage and took a seat. I turned his face towards mine then asked "How do you know Rufus, Timothy?" And just as he was about to answer, our three chorus directors walked in. Timothy got a little smirk on his face, kissed me on my forehead, and then gave the directors his undivided attention. *Dangit*! I would have to ask him at another time, but he had best believe, I was going to ask.

As I too gave my attention to the three chorus directors, I quickly learned that they were not to be played with! The way they operated you'd have thought they were getting paid a million dollars to teach us those spiritual songs. It would be after rehearsal that I would process their demand for perfection through spiritual eyes, because they were getting paid; they were building up treasure in heaven by using their earthly gifts.

All three reminded me of my dad because they accepted no excuses, especially since they knew we were all blessed with talents from above, so I was kinda use to their mentality. The first thing they did was split us up into groups, and low and behold, none other than Mr. Rufus himself was in mine. Go figure! And besides that, I didn't even think Rufus had it in him to sing nothing but that ghetto underground rap crap he always listened to when we were together, so Rufus making it into the chorus was a sight to behold.

Rufus wheeled himself right next to me. I wasn't fazed, not one bit. I could feel him looking at me but kept my attention on our director as she explained her expectations and went over the rules and regulations. She handed out binders that held every song we were to learn along with rehearsal times and locations. I felt a hand touch my thigh and let out a soft scream then jumped like I'd been bitten by a snake. It was Rufus and he thought he was slick. All eyes were on me as he asked "Can you get that piece of paper that fell for me please? I accidentally dropped it". All our paperwork was in three ring binders, so how'd that paper get out in the first place? I looked at Rufus for a long time before bending down to get it, and as I did I heard him whisper "Juicy". I snatched up the paper and handed it to him, and as I did he touched my hand and giggled. I yanked my hand back, gathered my stuff, and moved to another location.

After rehearsal, Timothy came over and asked if I was alright. Although in another group, he'd kept his eyes on me because of Rufus and had seen the whole paper incident. I told him that I was ok and that Rufus didn't faze me, then asked if he'd walk me to my dorm. Of course he obliged and as we walked out of the auditorium, and right past Rufus, he gave Timothy and me a head nod with an evil sinister smile on his face.

As soon as we exited the building I started talking about the chorus and the songs we were going to sing. I was so freaking hyped! At that moment I wasn't trying to talk about Rufus with Timothy or nobody else for that matter. That devil was a part of my past and I was just thankful I was able to be in the same room with him without having a panic attack.

With his arm thrown lazily around my shoulder, Timothy walked me to my dorm, and as he did, I silently thanked The Lord over and over again for this small victory that was given to me through His never ending mercies. Once we reached our destination I kissed Timothy on his forehead then went into my dorm and crashed.

A few hours later, Faith woke me up hysterical. I was in a deep, peaceful sleep when I heard her scream "Joanna! Joanna wake up! We gotta go to the hospital". With one eye opened, I groggily watched

Faith hop around our room with one leg in her pants trying to put on a shoe while blindly weeping. With the other eye still closed I leaned up on my elbow and said "Huh? What did you just say?" She repeated "The hospital! Hurry up! Timothy fell off his balcony, they don't know if he's going to make it." *WHAT THE HELL?!* I threw my blankets back and started hopping around with Faith, trying to get myself together while bursting into tears. *Timothy? I must be dreaming! We were just together a few hours ago! And what in the hell did she mean he may not make it? May not make what?* Faith and I managed to get on some clothes and shoes. We ran out of our dorm and hopped into a friend's truck that had been waiting on us. We were riding 10 deep, with everyone crying, trying to figure out what the hell had happened.

When we got to the hospital, the waiting room was already packed with students and faculty. We were updated with nothing because nobody knew anything. It was a waiting game. Two hours later, my parents, brothers, Timothy's parents and uncle were there. They must have really been trucking because the drive from our house was two hours, but they'd made it in one. About 10 minutes later I saw members of our congregation who were police men and women, walk through the door, which explained the fast timing. The officers from our city had called ahead to make sure both families had a police escort from their homes, directly to the hospital. When I saw my family walk through that door, Faith and I both ran into their outstretched arms. As my mother rubbed my head, I cried in her arms saying "Mommy, oh my God! Mooommy." She comforted me as best she could because my crying caused her to break down too. I loved my family. I ABSOLUTELY LOVED MY FAMILY!

Everyone eventually calmed down as we began to once again, play the torturous waiting game; and as we waited, we all silently prayed that our beloved Timothy would be alright.

The sun was rising when the doctors came out. They asked if they could speak with Timothy's parents alone, which caused his mother to breakdown. While holding his wife in his arms, Timothy's dad said "Whatever you have to say, say it now. These young folk have been here all night in vigil on behalf of our son. They have a right to know what's going on just as much as we do."

Some fellow students stood up so that the doctors could sit down. With a grave look on his face one introduced himself as the neurosurgeon who had worked on Timothy. My mind immediately went into shock mode. *Neurosurgeon? Timothy had been in surgery?* That bit of information explained the long wait. The doctor went on to say that Timothy's neck had been broken by the fall, and that if he hadn't landed~on the shrubbery, he would have died. My mind went into shock again as I thought *Timothy could have died? I can't believe one of my best friends could be dead at this very minute!* That was a very frightening thought to have, but it was a reality check on how serious the situation really was. But wait, he said that Timothy "Could have died", which meant my buddy was still alive! In my mind I started praising and thanking The Lord. Praising and thanking the Almighty God of miracles!

I listened intently as he went on to say that he had to fuse together some of Timothy's spine and vertebrae and as of yet, he didn't know if Timothy would ever walk again. Instead of everybody breaking down crying, they started praising God, because if walking again was Timothy's main issue, death as an alternative would have traumatize all our lives forever.

Another surgeon suggested that Timothy's parents limit visitation to immediate family, in order to keep the anguish of others from disturbing Timothy as he healed. He said that although the surgery was a success, Timothy's condition was still very critical and would be closely monitored for the next few weeks. After the physicians left, daddy said a prayer of praise because he knew, without a doubt, that The Lord had been very gracious to us all on that night, and he wanted us to thank Him for the precious gift of a saved life.

As people starting heading back to their dorms, I stuck around to give my support, as did my parents and brothers. When I could hold my lids opened no more, a fellow chorus member asked me if I wanted to ride back to the campus with them. Although Jonathan had offered to take me home, I opted out and decided to go with the chorus member. I felt that

Jonathan's presence was needed more at the hospital, rather than him wasting time chauffeuring me around, so I embraced everyone as I said my goodbyes.

I was beyond exhausted and took a cat nap during the ride home. When my foot hit campus soil, it was after 9 o'clock. I was hungry, stinky and just plain tired, but wanted to get a few hours of sleep in before I headed back out to the hospital later that afternoon, so I pushed all other needs to the side. By the time I reached my front door, my body ached so bad, that every step I took up the stairs felt like I was carrying 10 pound cement blocks on my legs, and the pain was excruciating.

I walked into my room and saw Faith was still knocked out. I couldn't even hate because the last few hours had been draining both mentally and physically. I flopped down onto my bed, stretched long and hard, and then closed my eyes. As I picked up a pillow to place on top of my head, I felt something scrape against my hand, but was too tired to lift my body up off the bed to see what it was. Instead, I slowly removed it from under my pillow. With my head facing sideways, I could see it was a white envelop that held a card, I lazily turned onto my back and then opened it. Neither the card nor the envelop had who it was from on them, and the sad thing is, I didn't need an introduction from the sender, because what I read on the inside of that card let me know that it was from the devil himself. In big, bold, black letters he had written "Don't fuck with me Juicy!" I scrambled out of my bed then out the front door. Once outside I looked to my left, and then to my right, trying to find Rufus. Although I was dead tired, I wasn't blind, and shouldn't have seconded guessed myself when I thought what I saw was legitimate as I walked to my front damn door!

Initially, I figured my eyes were playing tricks on me because of my exhaustion, when in actuality, they weren't. After we'd left the hospital, my chorus mate asked me if I needed her to stop at a store, or if I wanted to get something to eat. I told her no, although I was starving. I'd quickly pushed those hunger pains to the side, because my need for sleep superseded my bodies longing for nourishment, which is why I chose to go straight home. I was just too freakin' tired, and couldn't wait to get under my covers and fall asleep with the fan on blast. After being dropped off, I started speed walking towards my dorm, trying to expedite the joy of getting under my covers, but as I reached for my dorm door, I could have sworn I'd seen Rufus walking from behind that old oak tree, headed for his room. *How could that be if he was in a wheelchair?*

Although chocolate, I know that at that moment I turned snow white as I continued looking in both directions for Rufus, and then I felt a piercing cold chill run down my spine as it hit me. Timothy hadn't fallen off of his balcony, he had been pushed, and for some odd reason, I just knew he had been pushed by Rufus.

I slowly closed the front door and leaned against it with my eyes closed. I thought I was all cried out but soon found out that I wasn't. My tears burst forth like a calm never ending stream. *Had Rufus actually tried to kill my best friend, my brother in Christ, and one of my main sources of encouragement? Had he really just done that, over me?* That was a madness I couldn't comprehend. *Was it that freakin' deep?* Those thoughts scurried through my mind as I processed how evil Rufus actually was. It also caused me to wonder if his actions were out of love, obsession, or the fact that he loved the challenge, and that I posed a good one. In my eyes what he did was super petty, because he had always portrayed himself as a gutter, ruthless type nigga, when in actuality he was just a big limited cowered.

As I wiped the tears from my eyes, I pushed myself up off the front door and started heading up to my room, but before my foot could hit the first step, someone behind me had opened the entrance door. My heart skipped a beat because I was more than positive that it was Rufus coming to deal with me next. Just as I was about to make a mad dash to my room, I took a quick two second glance over my shoulder to get a view of who was crossing over my threshold, only to see that it was none other than my big hero of a brother, Jonathan.

I turned around and jumped into my big bros arms. He held me close as I again broke down into tears. I cried for a good fifteen minutes, and when the well had run dry, my big brother continued to hold me in his arms. In my mind I thought Jonathan had assumed I was crying over Timothy being in the hospital, when in reality I was crying over the fact that I'd put him there.

****

When I went to see Timothy the next day, I found out that his parents were sticking to the doctor's suggestion of limited visitors, and they were anal about it too. They had to turn a lot of people away, but were gracious enough to allow me to go in for a short visit. I was nervous about what I would see and wished that one of my brothers were there to escort me.

When I finally mustered up some courage and walked into Timothy's room I immediately put my hands over my mouth, hoping they would suppress the sound of my crying. *OH MY GOD!!!* I could not believe my eyes! Timothy was in what looked like a full body cast where the only things sticking out were his head, hands and feet. He had a tube going down his throat with a big machine connected to it. I would later learn that, that piece of equipment was providing Timothy's life support. I saw needles sticking out of what was visible of both his hands and one coming through the cast that was in his neck. As I looked at my friend my mind froze, *did I really cause all of this? What in the world have I done?*

I wanted to break down but didn't because I didn't want Timothy's parents to ask me to leave. I walked up to his bed and then looked down at my best friend. I felt like shit! Timothy had absolutely nothing to do with what was going on with me and Rufus! NOTHING! As I stood there looking down at my buddy I started to get mad. Almost to the point of rage. It was like my tears were sucked back up into my eyes because my face was as dry as the Red Sea when Moses led The Lords people across it. I was through entertaining Rufus's ass because this time, he'd gone too far.

I pulled up a chair and watched the monitors that were like a foreign language, trying to surmise what was going on inside my friend's body. After wasting my time doing that, I started softly singing, what a friend we have in Jesus. I took ahold of my friends hand and rubbed my thumb across his palm as I sang. I was really getting into the song when I felt a little twitch in one of his fingers which scared the hell out of me and caused me to jump up outta my chair. From what I had ear hustled from Timothy's parents, he was in a medically induced coma to rest his body so that the swelling on his spine could go down. That meant that he wasn't supposed to be able to move, so when he did, I was scared straight.

I guess I must have let out a little scream because his parents calmly walked in to see if I was alright. All I could do was point as I stood shell shocked at what had just happened. I felt Timothy's mom place her hand on my back and start rubbing it. When I could get my voice, I hoarsely whispered "He moved, Timothy moved his hand." His parents gracefully made their way to his bedside and sat down. His mother took the hand I'd been holding and started caressing it. Over her shoulder she patiently said "Of course he moved Joanna, we have half the world petitioning The Lord on behalf of our baby. We belong to the King honey, which means no matter what the outcome may be, we already got the victory".

As I watched Timothy's parents lovingly look at their son, I quietly made my exit, saddened by the fact that if it wasn't for me, they wouldn't be in this situation. When I'd initially made my way into Timothy's room, and beheld the condition of my friend, at that moment I'd told myself that it was time for me to take some action. There was no way I could live my life dancing in circles trying to evade the inevitable, because no matter how hard I tried, it seemed as if the shadow of misery was always on my heels. Taking some action was in order, which meant that it was time for me to confront the devil himself, Rufus.

Chapter Three

~Rufus~

Where's yo sword at little Miss Christian? Didn't yo daddy tell you to never declare war without your armor on, especially when battling evil...you's a dumb bitch!

After my visit with Timothy, I was dropped back off at the campus, and as soon as the family friend pulled off, I pulled out my phone and called Rufus. Once again, he answered on half a ring, as if he had been expecting my call. Before he could say anything sly, I asked him to meet me in fifteen minutes at the auditorium where the chorus auditions were held so that we could talk. I hung up before he could reply, and started footing it in that direction.

I didn't know what I was going to say, but I knew this madness had to stop. As I walked towards the auditorium, I said a quick prayer because I knew exchanging spit with the devil wasn't going to be an easy task.

Angela Moore

As I watched Rufus approach, walking, I couldn't find anything about him attractive. How I had gotten so caught up in this crazy boys life I'll never know because what I saw was an empty shell with a heart that was corroded, sad, and without hope. When he got within a couple of feet of me I held up my hand, closed my eyes, said another quick prayer, and then told Rufus, "That's close enough". He smirked, put his hands in his pockets, rattled his change, and then started rocking back and forth on his heels.

I looked him in his eyes and felt nothing but sadness. He had no clue about life, and was so stuck on getting who and what he wanted, that he was missing out on all the beautiful things God wanted for him. I've thought, on more than one occasion, about how The Lord could use Rufus in so many powerful ways for the good of humanity. When I was having my "Rendezvous" with Rufus, naw, let me keep it real, when I was "Swimming in the sea of sin" with Rufus, I found out he knew a whole lotta people who went for bad. At the time I was so caught up that, that piece of information flew right over my head, but after I had removed myself from that abyss of darkness, I was able to see things a whole lot clearer. I was a living testimony to what the song amazing grace says, 'I once was lost but now I'm found, was blind but now I see' because that's exactly how it happened. While with Rufus, I couldn't see a thing. I couldn't see how dark he was, how he functioned in a dark cloud that blew him wherever it wanted him to go. How he was an

41

instrument used by the devil to devour my soul, or how he allowed the god of materialism and greed to reign over his life. I thanked God that He had removed the scabs of lies from my eyes and had allowed me to see that the cloud of evil that stayed above Rufus's head, and engulfed his entire body, and had no problem spreading its love of wickedness towards me.

I took in a deep breath and said "Rufus, I'm not scared of you" and before I could get the next word out he replied "You should be". Those words pissed me off! I put my hand on my hip, turned my head to the side and then squinted my eyes as I looked at him. I thought *let me shut this down right quick!* and then answered "Why Rufus? Why should I be scared of you, because you're evil? Huh? Is that why? So you think you a big boy because you put my best friend in the hospital? Huh Rufus? So you bad now huh? That makes you hard and a man. You ain't nothing Rufus! Nothing but a worker for the devil! And why in the world are you here? Why did you come to a Christian college? Or better yet, why did you FOLLOW ME to a Christian college? Don't you have a baby to attend too?" When I said that his smirk got bigger. Like he didn't know I knew about that. I said "Yeah, how'd that work out for you? Huh? Walking around having babies and chasing me all around town. Do you know how sad that looks? And it makes you look weak! Leave me alone Rufus, would you please just leave me alone? I don't want anything to do with you ever again. You have brought nothing but bad into my life and The Lord has replaced it with His goodness, so the battle is already won."

For some stupid reason, everything I had been through with him came to the surface of my mind, especially what had happened to Timothy, and I burst into tears. I started yelling "You see?! You see what you've done to me?! I have tried so hard not to hate you Rufus, because I know I can't go to heaven with hate on my heart, but you are making that so damn hard! I hate that I ever met you! I hate that I hid you from my family! I hate that I put you before The Lord, I hate that I ever called you Rufus! I HATE THAT I EVER MET YOOOU!!!" Rufus stood there, still rocking and rattling his change. I started wiping my tears away with the sleeve of my shirt. I took a deep breath, said another prayer, and then asked, in a sad tired voice, "Rufus, could you please just leave me alone? Just leave me alone Rufus, please."

Rufus continued standing there in thought, not saying anything in return. I dropped my shoulders and head, then started heading back to my dorm realizing that I had wasted my time and energy talking to a brick wall. That moment had drained me dry, and I was tired. What little bit of fight I had left in me was depleted. After I had walked a few feet, in a calm steady voice Rufus said "Hey Juicy, call Tamara and ask her how my baby doin'". I couldn't believe what the hell I'd just heard and turned around so fast I twisted my ankle then fell to the ground. I looked at Rufus in total shock as I grabbed my foot in agony, and started rocking back and forth on my butt. *Oh my goodness! Ouch! Ouch! Ouch!* My ankle hurt so dang on bad a tear slid out my eye! In no time the pain had traveled up my leg, and through my torso, to my brain which caused me to feel as if my head and ankle were about to explode! Even in all that agony my mind couldn't quite wrap itself around what he said, *did this boy just tell me to call my cousin Tamar? Is he talking about one of my Aunt B's daughters? Rufus has a baby by my freaking first cousin?* The confusion on my face caused Rufus to smile as he blew me a kiss, turned and then walk into the shadows.

I sat on the ground for a long time crying for my ankle and for what Rufus had just told me. *My cousin Tamar has a baby by Rufus? How in the hell did that happen? And how in the hell did that slip past me? Were Aunt B and her kids so greedy that they would risk a relationship with me to continue to get stuff since I wasn't around to give them my things anymore? What kind of family does that to each other? Over stuff that don't amount to anything?* The sad thing is, I had willingly given them all that Rufus had given me, but now they were taking what Rufus had to offer, by any means necessary. I know I shouldn't have been surprised because Aunt B and her girls were always out for self, but Tamara, we were like sisters. We were like fucking sisters!

I took the jacket I had on off, and wrapped it around my ankle for support. I then slowly stood on my good foot, while applying a very small amount of pressure to the other. As soon as I tried to hop in the direction of my dorm I fell. I silently prayed I rolled onto my stomach to get into position to crawl on my hands and knees. I then slowly pulled my knees up to my chest. My ankle hurt so bad I plopped back down onto my stomach, then started crying again. I put my head into my arms and wept. I felt so damn hopeless I almost fell asleep on the filthy ground consumed with grief over too much information.

After a few minutes, I heard someone approaching me from behind, and when I twisted my neck around and looked up, I saw that it was Rufus. I didn't pay him any attention and laid my head back down. My lids and heart were heavy as I welcomed sleep but was awakened when I felt him nudge me with his foot. I didn't move. He said "Get yo ass up Juicy, yo damn ankle might be broke". I didn't say nothin', I just broke down and cried. I covered my ears but was still able to hear him say "I ain't gon' offer to help yo ass no more, so you better get the hell up". I flipped onto my back, accumulated as much saliva as I could, and then spit in Rufus's face. As he stepped back I saw something very dark replace that silly smirk he had previously worn, which caused me to feel a little fear.

I quickly flipped out my cell phone and called Faith. I told her where I was and that I needed her to come help me to our dorm. The whole time Faith and I were talking, Rufus and I stared each other down, barely blinking. I hung up the phone, laid on my back, put my arm over my face and didn't say another word to that devil. Although my eyes were closed, I knew he was still there because I hadn't heard him walk away. About five minutes after the call, I could hear someone running towards me, so I lifted my head and saw Faith's shadow approaching and felt a huge relief. When I looked back at Rufus, I saw that he was looking from me to Faith and vice versa. He put that sly smirk back on his face, spit on the ground, and then walked away.

When Faith had finally made it to my side, and beheld my sad predicament, she could not believe what she saw. I was a dirty hot mess. She bent down and gently placed my arm over her head and across her shoulders, then helped me to my feet. As we headed towards our dorm, I had to hop on one foot with my other leg bent at the knee, so that my damaged one wouldn't touch the ground. But even that careful move caused me a whole lotta pain. It took us a good thirty minutes to get me into the dorm and tucked in bed. A walk and a task that should have normally taken a few minutes.

I laid down and popped some ibuprofen while Faith got a wet face towel, put some ice in it, and placed it on my swollen ankle. She had tried to take my shoe off, but when I started crying out in pain, she aborted that mission. As I laid there I prayed that my ankle wasn't broken because although the campus wasn't big, when working with a hurt or possibly broken ankle, it made the campus look as if it was larger than two football fields. *How in the world was I going to get to my classes in this state?* I was going to have to come up with a plan B, but at the same time come up with a good excuse to tell my parents on how I hurt myself.

It seemed as if everything that had to do with Rufus always led to pain and anguish for me. In the back of my mind I knew he wasn't going to give up. That boy had never been told no by anybody, and I knew he wasn't going to start now. It was the principle of the matter, not necessarily because he loved or even wanted to be with me. He just refused to end up on the bottom. And because of that, his selfishness would cause me turmoil for a very long time.

After some of the swelling in my ankle went down, Faith went back into the bathroom to ring out the face towel and placed more ice in it, but this time when she came back she asked "Now who was that guy I saw walking away from you when I walked up?" As soon as she asked the question my head started to hurt. I didn't even answer, I just laid in that bed thinking about all the things that had transpired over the last few days, which caused my headache to turn into a migraine.

My head was pounding so hard I tried shutting all thoughts of Rufus out of it. To accomplish that task, I shifted my focus to things that were pure and gentle and holy, which caused me to start falling off to sleep. Although I wanted to keep my eyes opened so I could deal with my possibly broken ankle issue, I couldn't, especially since I'd placed my mind on good things and not Rufus, which had kept me up many of nights. I realized I was more tired than what I thought, so I stopped fighting the urge and allowed sleep to win out. I blurrily saw Faith sitting at the foot of my bed, nursing my ankle, and just before my head started to nod, I heard myself answer her question as I whispered "The devil" and then drifted off to sleep.

Angela Moore

Chapter Four

~Rufus~

You think that niggas an angel? Shit, his ass got black wings just like me.

I went to see Timothy every single day, hurt ankle and all. And it wasn't because of guilt it was because I truly had love for my brother in Christ. I would catch a ride up to the hospital with whoever I could, but as the days turned into weeks, and the weeks into months, the rides started to dwindle right along with people visiting.

I spoke with my family daily and kept them abreast of Timothy's condition. I had also formed a very tight bond with Timothy's parents, and would touch bases with them while also keeping them informed of any changes in Timothy if for some reason they couldn't make it out for a visit. But every time I spoke with my folks, I would complain to them about how hard of a task it was becoming for me to make my daily visits to see my best friend

49

due to transportation issues, and that's how it was decided that it was time for me to get my own car, a decision my parents and brothers made, not me.

My mom and dad had talked it over with Jude and Jonathan, and all four concluded that it was well overdue. Although my parents were the ones who were going to purchase me a vehicle, Jude and Jonathan had insisted that they get me my first car, especially since I would be using it as a means of ministry. Of course Jude wanted to be super cheap, which made Jonathan pissed! But once Jonathan asked him "So that means, when that piece of junk you wanna get her breaks down, you gon hit the dusty and musty roads to go give her a jump, cause you know she always crying broke". Jonathan said Jude had the nerve to say "Let me pray on it". *What!? Pray on what, common sense?* After Jonathan gave Jude a look that said "Nigga! Are you serious!?", Jude relented and helped pay for me a 2009 Toyota Corolla, versus the 1989 Toyota Corolla Jude wanted to get me. When Jonathan told me that I thought *Really Jude? Are you freaking serious?* Sometimes his cheapness didn't make no crazy sense. God knows I loved my big brother, but sometimes, sometimes, sometimes!

The whole car situation turned out to be a big surprise, because after worship one Sunday, as I was visiting Timothy at the rehab facility that he'd been transferred to, I looked up and saw my parents and brothers walk in. Every now and then all four of them would come check up on me and Timothy, but not all four at the same time. By then, Timothy had gained major mobility back into his limbs, and as of yet, he wasn't walking by himself, but he was well on his way to a full recovery. Timothy and I were in the rec room playing the Wii game the facility used to help their patients with physical therapy, and although Timothy couldn't fully use his legs, he could sure use his arms and would beat me every time. I told him that if he kept it up he was going to be walking around like those cartoon characters with a big upper body and little bitty legs and that would not get him far with the ladies, sanctified or not.

Timothy had just raised his arms in victory when I looked up and saw my whole family walk through the recreation room door. I dropped my control and ran into by big brothers arms, then into my parents. It wasn't until then that I realized how much I missed my family. Not the individuals of my family, but the family unit as a whole. The Sunday dinners, the hustle and bustle as we got ready for school, Jude getting super-hot as he watched me and Jonathan eat cereal on a Saturday morning as he held the almost empty milk carton that had only a corner of milk left in it. Those were the things I missed, everyday life with my family.

Everybody went over to Timothy and chatted it up with him for about 30 minutes. As they talked, I found the friend who had given me a ride, and let them know that they could cut out if they wanted, because my family would be driving me back to school. Although most of our mutual friends had gone back to everyday life, we still had a few who hung in there with Timothy's slow to us, but fast to the staff, progression. That in itself was a huge blessing because otherwise, I'd have to catch the bus to see my friend every day, which was time consuming and costly. Yeah, my family laced my pockets with plenty of coins, but the majority of the money was actually used on school, and I didn't want to burden them with any extra. I was growing up, so I needed to act like it.

After a quick visit, my parents and brothers said their goodbyes to Timothy as I gave him my traditional kiss on the forehead and told him that I'd see him tomorrow. As we exited the facility, my parents started heading towards their car, while Jude and Jonathan went in the direction of a car I didn't recognize. When Jude opened the driver's door, I stopped in my tracks, put my hand on my hip then asked "Who's ride is this?", and before Jude could answer Jonathan answered for the both of them and said "Jude's" with a smirk on his face. I folded my arms across my chest and said "Reeeally? You mean to tell me that Jude, for the first time in his life, finally bought something halfway decent for himself besides suites and food?" Jude looked at me like "Now see, I knew I shouldn't have broken the budget for her butt" but at that time, I hadn't known that Jude had broken his budget for me, so I lit into his frugal behind.

As I started getting into the car Jude said, "Be quiet Bug and get yo butt into this car" while sliding in himself. When Jonathan got into the back seat, I should a known something was up, but I was still stuck on the fact that Jude had actually spent some coins.

My parents were behind us as Jude drove me home, and during the whole ride I was pushing on buttons while asking Jude retarded questions like "Now you do know this is called a CD player right?" Or going ham on him about the simplicity of sacrifice "Did you get yourself a car charger? It won't use up any of your gas if that's what you're worried about, but it might tap into yo battery a little bit. But you still need to get one just in case you get stuck on the side of the road and your phone is dead. Oh! My bad, you've got a halfway decent ride so you shouldn't be stuck on the side of the road should you?" Jonathan was in the back seat cracking up as I put in, then took out, the numerous CDs they'd bought for me, while jokingly explaining to Jude how to use the CD player.

When we pulled up to my dorm, Jude had barely stopped the car before I'd hopped out and ran up to my parents ride so that they could come up to my room, but when they didn't get out, I leaned into their truck and asked them what was up. Mommy said they needed to head back home because daddy was tired. I was a little disappointed when she said that, but saved face because I didn't want daddy to feel bad about leaving me. I gave both of them a kiss then noticed Jonathan and Jude opening the back doors to my parents SUV. I stood there confused as

Jude rolled down his back window and said "Use it
to the glory of God Ladybug, you deserve it" then
held out the keys to what I thought were keys to his
car, towards me. I said, "Huh?" He repeated "Here,
these are for you. We had a family meeting and felt
that it was time for you to have your own wheels.
God has been providing for you to get back and
forth to visit Timothy, but we know that there were a
few times you almost didn't make it because of
transportation. Well, now you don't have to worry
about that anymore. Here, take these keys, they're
for you." I know my face was super ugly, but I didn't
care. I broke down like I was a kid again. Face all
scrunched up and everything. Mama and my
brothers got out of the car and hugged me, while
daddy tried to play hard, as if they had to leave
pronto, and he stayed in the car. I knew it had to be
the hand of Jesus that had touched my daddy's heart
to allow me to get a car, because daddy had barely
let me get a driver's license.

When Jude and Jonathan would complain about
having to take me everywhere, they would gently let
daddy know that I could be taking myself, if only he
would let go. When daddy didn't budge, mommy put
in a good word for me during some pillow talk, and
that's the only reason he relented. But as usual, he
had some conditions. Unlike Jonathan and Jude, I
had to take drivers education, and when it came to
the driving portion, daddy had to be in the car with
me, which everyone knows is against the rules. So
by me getting a car was a present day miracle.

I ran over to daddy's side of the car with my arms stretched out like I was learning how to walk. I reached inside and kissed him a thousand times while telling him thank you all over his face. Yeah, I was still crying, but when I looked into my daddy's eyes, I kissed a little tear that was creeping out of the corner of one of his. I took my nose and put it on his and did the wiggle, wiggle, wiggle, the way we did when I was a little girl. His baby was growing up, and that was a hard pill for him to swallow. I gave him one more kiss then started jumping up and down like I was on The Price is Right.

Jude and Jonathan had gotten back into my parents truck while I was doing the mushy, mushy with daddy, but got back out as my mom got back in. They started talking to me about the car as we walked towards it. Outta the blue Jonathan's attention was shifted and he said "I'll be riiiiight back" then went behind my dorm. Jude continued to tell me about my ride, but I saw him stiffen a little bit when Jonathan had said those words. I noticed both of their behavior, but didn't notice at the same time, because I was hanging on to every word that came outta Jude's mouth about my new ride.

We both got into the car, and I had to listen as Jude micromanaged my driving skills, although we were freaking parked! I listened patiently because I felt kinda bad for dogging my big bro out for buying a decent ride, so I pushed buttons and turned the steering wheel while he went on and on about nothing. I wanted to cut him off so bad, but didn't, and was super happy when I saw Jonathan jogging from the back of my building, then head straight for my parents truck, which was a godsend.

I opened the driver's door fast and hard then bounced, a big fat hint for Jude to get out. As I walked towards my parent's truck I looked over my shoulder at Jude, and saw he had a disappointed look on his face because I hadn't let him finish. I smiled and waved him towards mommy and daddy, but when I turned back around I rolled my eyes up in my head because Jude could be overkill at times. Just as I made it to the truck, I thought I saw Rufus out of my peripheral. It looked like he was kinda bent over, walking from behind my dorm. I thought *you's a bad nigga if you that bold,* and then chatted it up with my folks until Jude got his hurt feelings together and got out my ride. I quickly looked Jonathan over, and hadn't notice anything about him that was different, until my eyes skimmed over his bloodied knuckles curled up into a fist. He tried to hurry up and hide them in a bandana, but it was too late, I had already seen them. I said my finial goodbye, cried some more, and waved to them as they drove off yelling instructions to me out of their windows.

When they were out of view, I stood there looking at my dorm. Most young college students would have ran straight to their new ride, and hit the road. But naw, not me. My big bro don't make no moves unless they make sense, so while gripping my car keys in my hand, I slowly made my way to the back of my building.

I stood in one spot and carefully looked around at my surroundings and from where I was standing, nothing looked outta order. But then I started walking around the area, kicking some rocks here and there, and that's when I started seeing small drops of blood scattered throughout the ground. I followed the blood trail, and the further I walked, the more blood I saw. When I came to what looked like a huge blood clot, I thought *that's what the fuck you get!*

Although I know it was bad for me to think, I couldn't help myself, especially since I was witnessing Timothy's struggle on a day by day bases. My best friend had almost lost his life because of Rufus's selfish ways so some payback was in order.

I shifted my eyes from the ground and started looking around the property again. Deep down I had a feeling that Rufus was somewhere watching. I stared back down at that clot, spit on it, and then met Rufus's eyes as he stepped from behind a tree. He was holding his side as we stared at each other, our silence speaking volumes. His ass was breathing real hard with sweat dripping from his face. I wondered why he hadn't gone to the hospital, especially with a big fat clot that was extracted from his body on the ground. Then I realized that his ass was such a control freak that he'd risk his own life to make a point. When I couldn't stand looking at him anymore, I turned around, excited to take my new ride back up to the hospital to show my best friend.

As I drove to the rehab facility, I praised The Lord for that car! I know my friends didn't mind taking me to visit Timothy, but it was a big burden for me to ask, and at times I hated too, but because of my love for my homie, I humbled myself and did what I had to do to get to my buddy. But now! Shooooot, it was on!

As I walked into Timothy's room, I held my keys in front of my face, shaking them between my thumb and index finger. His butt hopped up like he could walk and fell straight to the floor. Of course he was not about to embarrass himself, so as he headed towards that tiled surface, he stretched out his arms and landed in a push-up position. *Who freakin' does that!?* When he started going up and down, doing real push-ups, we howled on the floor laughing.

****

Timothy's parents had decided to leave him close to campus, instead of taking him home to be closer to them. For years they had listened to him speak on being about His Fathers business, so when they saw how fast he was progressing, they made the choice to leave him there as a means of encouragement to move forward in his passion for Christ, in spite of his limitations.

We were in our second year and Timothy had gotten behind in his studies, but primarily at the beginning of our third semester. Thankfully I hadn't, considering all the stress and pain I had endured knowing that Rufus had done this to my friend. Whenever I would look back over my life, I knew it had to be The Lord who kept me because the average person would have dropped out or transferred to a school closer to home, but not me. My parents had instilled in me a tenacity that allowed me to believe that I was more than a conquer in Jesus Christ, and although at times something deep within me wanted to throw in the towel and give up, God's love and purpose for my life kept me going.

It was a given that Timothy and I were both out of the chorus, but we didn't give two hoots about that. He was alive, and that's all that mattered. Once he was able to be taken off the life support, and we witnessed his miraculous progression, we made up our own songs of praise to our God of many mercies. At end of the semester, although I didn't make the dean's list, I still had a high GPA, and of course my parents understood. Timothy on the other hand was naturally withdrawn from his lessons right after the accident, but the president of the school knew Timothy's accident wasn't caused by alcohol or drugs, so he gave Timothy a clean slate and erased those classes from his schedule as if they never existed. Since that surprise visit from my family, I hadn't seen Rufus, and to be honest, I was so wrapped up in Timothy that Rufus was actually a forgotten thought, but with Rufus being Rufus, he demanded my attention, and the next entrance he made would be a grand one, and the true beginning of my demise.

Because of Timothy's situation, I opted to stay on campus during school breaks so that I could be a witness to The Lords great powers as he healed my friend from the bondage of inability and limitations. Limitations the doctors said he would have for a lifetime. Timothy was slowly becoming a living testimony to the world, because as his doctors said no, Our God said yes, and no amount of medical doctors could overrule that verdict, not even the best neurologist in the world. And although Faith's reasons for staying on campus during the breaks was different from ours, she was still a great support system for both Timothy and I.

****

Faiths circumstances were a whole lot different from mine, and because of the financial hardship her family had endured to send her to college, her going home on every break would have thrown her family into a worse financial situation than they were already in. But then, a miracle happened.

My parents came up with the idea of renting a little two bedroom house that was located on the campus grounds, so that Faith and I wouldn't be the only two young ladies staying in the dorms roaming around the school grounds alone. My parents didn't think it was safe nor appropriate, so while trying to figure out how to handle the issue, mommy had remembered a house that she'd read about in the schools welcome packet, a house that just happened to be located behind the campus police office. Of course the idea sounded great to Faith and I, but her parents couldn't get past the fact that my family had willingly volunteered to take on most of the cost. Faith's family knew they weren't stacked up, but they still had their dignity, and didn't want to burden anyone with their responsibility. They figured that The Lord had provided for them thus far, and believed He would continue to do so. My dad had spoken to Faith's dad on more than one occasion letting him know that the money wasn't an issue, but the safety of their girls were. Faith's dad knew that if she didn't move into the house, our living apart would only intensify our lack of safety. At least with the two of us together, if need be, we could try to fight off an intruder, but one on one would most likely be a losing battle. Faith's dad finally said yes, but only under the condition that everything be split 50/50, so the deal was set.

The house we were moving in too had been erected in memory of one of the original founding fathers of the college. Although it was usually used to house someone on the faculty, from the start of the school year up to that point it had been vacant and not needed. Word had spread fast about Faith and I staying in our dorm during our breaks, so when daddy solicited the president of the school with inquiries, plans were put into motion, and two weeks later, Faith and I had our very own living space.

The house came completely furnished, which was a bonus because neither one of us had any coins for anything "Extra". Other than our bed linen, nothing else was needed. Our parents let it be known off the top that absolutely no one was to stay the night. Daddy, on moving day, with a very stern look said "Boys isn't a topic we should have to mention, now is it?" The way my daddy said that caused Faith and I to subconsciously and automatically grab for each other's hand as our eyes got big and we shook our heads no.

Faith's parents couldn't afford the expense of visiting to make sure everything was on the up and up, so in good faith, they trusted my parents to do so. While daddy was chatting it up on school grounds with the campus president, mommy took Faith and I to lunch and shopping. We really didn't need anything but mommy insisted on purchasing bathroom decorations and little nick knacks for the kitchen. She even threw in some plants to place throughout the house saying "You should always have a piece of Gods beautiful green goodness around ya house. Just as His plants need the sun to sustain life, you need The Son to sustain yours, so placing plants throughout the house is just a little reminder." In couldn't help but think *where does she come up with these simple yet profound analogies?*

It was at times like that, that I realized how blessed I was to have a God fearing mother.

After shopping, mommy floated around our little house like a butterfly, making sure everything was as it should be. And by the time daddy had come to pick her up and say his own goodbyes, she was like a proud mama bear as she stood in our front doorway, with her hands in front of her face in a praying position, looking at her handy work.

After they'd left, Faith and I held hands and started jumping around in circles, screaming like two year olds. Once we calmed down we popped some microwave popcorn, compliments of the groceries mommy bought, sat on the couch and started watching some TV. We were both yawning at about the same time and it was only 8 o'clock at night. Faith and I both had packed class schedules and would always hit the sack early, but with that being our first night in our own little spot, we tried to put our big girl panties on and hang with the big dogs. Not happening. Faith turned off the TV, and as I was about to get up off the couch, she took ahold of my arm and said "Joanna, I just want to say thank you for everything. You have been better to me than my own sister and I want you to know that I appreciate that. I've watched you as you ministered to Timothy and everyone that comes into your circle without giving it any thought. You, my friend, are a very beautiful person with a very beautiful heart, and I want you to know that I love you, and thank you for your kindness".

I almost started crying. It never occurred to me that people took notice of the things I did for others, and in reality, I never looked for any accolades for the things I did because I did things from the heart, not for recognition. I only wanted to please The Lord and if people took notice of my good works because of that, then so be it, because as long as The Lord was happy, I was happy. I gave Faith a real tight hug and thanked her for her kind words. And if I wasn't so tired I'd have stayed up and talked to her for a while, but with all the excitement, mommy and daddy coming to visit I was pooped.

I went to my bedroom, put a pillow on the hardwood floor and got down on my knees. While in a praying position I thought *dang, I shoulda hit mommy up for a couple more pillows. I'll try to remember next time,* and then fell asleep while thanking The Lord for His goodness.

****

Faith and I were back on our school grind, and nothing had really changed from our habits at the dorm. It was the same crap, different location. During one of my visits with Timothy, I felt it was time to talk about that humongous pink elephant that no one wanted to speak on, Rufus. I decided it would be after one of his physical therapy sessions, and although I knew he would be exhausted, I couldn't hold back any longer.

Timothy's physical therapist had started his walking regimen. It was tedious work, and at times I'd find myself trying to will his legs to move as his therapist cheered him on. One day I was so into it, that as Timothy slowly lifted his left leg, I was slowly lifting mine too, then all of a sudden he dropped his leg, and so did I. When I looked up at him in disappointment, I found him staring at me like? And we started cracking up laughing. I held up my hands in surrender, and then went to his room to take a seat.

As I waited, I flicked through channels on his TV although I wasn't really trying to find anything. I was trying to figure out a way to broach the subject of Rufus. I guess The Lord felt a little compassion for me, because after Timothy was wheeled to his room and placed in his bed, he put the burden of speaking of Rufus on Timothy's shoulders.

As was our habit, after he was in bed, I lifted his arm, placed it lovingly around my neck, and then scooted next to him all comfy like. But instead of arguing over what movie to watch, or helping him with his school work, he turned the TV off and Timothy asked me to sit facing him. I did as I was asked and just when I was about to speak on the subject of Rufus, he prompted the subject by asking, "You wanna know how this happened?" I shook my head up and down but was thinking *THANK YOU JESUS!!!* And so he began.

"I'd left you at your dorm and was walking towards mine. I was really hyped about shifting through the songs and itinerary that the chorus director had given us". Timothy stopped, looked out his bedroom window, then randomly said "I knew not to trust that nigga, and he had better be glad he caught me slippin', otherwise our roles would be reversed" I stopped him right there and asked "What do you mean you knew not to trust him? How do you even know he's not to be trusted?" Timothy looked back at me and was about to spill the beans, but stopped himself. Instead he said "Don't worry about all that, and don't stop me no more, ok Joanna." I sat there in total shock. Timothy had never, ever talked to me like that. I started to give him some neck and hand on the hip action, but thought better of it because for some reason, I knew this would be Timothy's first, and last time ever speaking on what had happened that night, and I didn't want to mess it up. I said "Ok" in as nice a voice as I could muster, then proceeded to get not one, but many shocks of my life.

"It was dark and I could feel something wasn't right, but like I said, I was caught up. It was eerily quiet, but that was something I realized after the fact, as I laid in my hospital bed night after night. I went to my dorm room which was on the third floor, something you wouldn't know because you've never been there. But anyway, I sat at my desk and started looking through the chorus paperwork. I knew my roommate was on the balcony because I could hear him on the phone talking to his girl. About 15 minutes later he bounced, and although I didn't look up, I knew he was gone. About 10 minutes after that I heard some rambling out on the balcony. In my mind I thought 'didn't he just leave?' and I didn't go out to investigate, but after I heard more noise, I stood up, opened the balcony door, and stuck my head out. I looked to my left, then right, and didn't see anything, but as I was pulling back to shut the door I saw the reflection of a belt buckle. I walked out and asked what was up. I already knew who it was so I figured we'd go on and set everything out on the table. I also knew that if that nigga climbed his ass up three stories, he sure in the hell didn't come to talk."

When Timothy said that I raised an eyebrow *is this my sweet, little nerdy Carlton acting Timothy? My little preacher man?* I sat there in shock because I had never, ever heard this side of Timothy!

I guess he saw my mind wondering because he laughed and said "What? You didn't think I had a little gangsta in me? I'm sanctified, not stupid. Look Joanna, on a serious note, I grew up on the mean streets of Chicago, where over time, bullets and microwave popcorn merged together and made the same sound. From the time I could walk to school by myself, to the time I left for college, I've walked over more dead bodies than you can count, trying to get an education. While in the third grade I lost my best friend to gun violence in a drive by shooting, so I've been crying tears of sorrow for years. Because of where I lived, I had no choice in growing up fast, the streets of Chicago made that a mandatory necessity, like breathing air. I learned some hard lessons about those mean streets, but when I walked home from the bus stop, every single day it was like I was walking home to a small piece of heaven. My home life and the church were the only places I found peace. Not that superficial peace you be hearing those liars on TV talking about either, I mean real peace Joanna. Peace in my mom's embrace when every day she held me close as I walked through the front door from school, thanking The Lord I made it home alive. All the way up to when I was a senior in high school. And you know what, most young men would shun that type of behavior, saying they didn't want to be labeled a mama's boy, but not me. Naw, I loved my mama and her prayers, so that wasn't up for discussion in my world."

I was in shock of the things that were coming out of my friend's mouth! It just goes to show that you never really know a person until you get to really know a person. Appearances are oh so very deceiving. Timothy continued by saying "Although those streets could have made me hard as cement, the love and compassion I watched my parents display in that abyss of evil proved otherwise. My parents never made excuses for wickedness, but they helped as many people as they could on a daily basis. I recall a day when all kinds of madness was going on at the park across the street from our apartment. As usual, the everyday music of the shots and sirens started to play. Daddy and I were at the kitchen table eating dinner when we heard loud banging on our front door. As mama started walking towards the door to open it, daddy yelled 'Don't you open that front door woman!', but mama could feel the urgency on the other side and started unlocking the 7 deadbolts that kept us safe from the outside world. When she cracked opened our front door, the neighborhood drug dealer was standing on the other side, holding his blood soaked chest with one hand, and a newborn baby with the other. With sweat running down his face he said 'Please ma'am, please', threw the baby into my mother's arms, took two steps back and then dropped dead.

Mama closed our door, put the bolts back on, and then looked down into the most beautiful pair of green eyes she'd ever seen." I screamed "WHAT!?" He started laughing, and then said "Yep, that little green eyed sister of mine was the major dope kingpin in our hoods daughter." I was freaking speechless. *Oh my goodness!* That little girl was the pride and joy of their family, and the sweetest little angel you would ever want to come across, so I guess that's why his parents gave her that name. The crazy thing is, you couldn't even tell she wasn't blood. It was like God had placed her in a family where she would never have to guess if she belonged, because if nobody ever told her she was adopted, she would have never known.

Once he realized I'd gotten over my shock, Timothy continued by saying "Ya see, after my mom gave birth to me, my parents found out she had

69

ovarian cancer, so that was the beginning of the end of their child bearing opportunities, that is, until God gave us Angel. Anyway, that's a little bit of how I came to have a little street savvy in me Joanna. It's not something I asked for, it was something I was forced to take, and I thank God for it because before that punk made that weak move and pushed me over the balcony, I was whipping his ass". Huh? That was a quick shift of topics. Timothy said "Yeah, I wanted to talk to him man to man, and at first, that's what we were doing, until I told him that I would die to protect the girl I loved". I squinted my eyes so tight they started to hurt, I then whispered "What?" Timothy burst out laughing. He was laughing so hard and long he started holding his side, but I didn't see nothing funny.

Timothy was in love with me? That was a bit too much for me to handle, so I started getting up off the bed. I was about to tell Timothy that we'd finish the conversation on another day, but before I was able to completely get up, while still laughing, he grabbed my arm and pulled me back down. He said "Chill Joanna. It's all good. I know you don't feel the same way about me, and I'm cool with that. I've managed to keep my feelings for you on the low low because I'd rather have you as a true friend, than risk perusing you and end up with nothing at all". Now that was deep! Wow, I never knew. Timothy's butt was mature as hell. Dang, kinda made me wish I could force myself to like him because the boy I was looking at was going to be a phenomenal, God fearing man, for some phenomenal, God fearing woman.

I looked my best friend in his eyes and leaned in close. I put my hands on the side of his face and put my forehead on his. I felt his hands go around my waist and pull me closer. I slowly closed my eyes and placed my lips on his. I felt his hands shake a little as he pulled me to his chest, and took the kiss deeper. *Omgosh! This boy can kiss!* We explored the newness of each other for a good five minutes, and when Timothy heard me moan, he pulled back, but just a little. I started going in for round two but he stopped me. I sat back, and once again looked into his eyes. I saw a whole lotta different emotions come across his face, but the strongest one was love. Followed by that, I saw sadness, because my eyes confirmed that I didn't love him back, not in the way that he loved me. I averted my gaze because they told the truth, but Timothy took his index finger and put it under my chin, forcing me to look at him. In a soft voice he asked "One more for the road?" I put a small smile on my face, and shook my head up and down. He again put his hands on my back, caressing it, trying to feel as much of me as he could. He then pulled me close and placed his soft lips on mine. We kissed like new lovers, and when he heard me moan again, he broke the kiss and then held me close.

We sat there in silence, holding each other, basking in the moment, because we both knew we would never embrace like that again. To cut through the thickness of the seriousness, Timothy said "I got some Mentos in my nightstand, you might wanna get one", I leaned back and we started cracking up as I pushed him on his head. I loved that boy, I really did.

As we got back into our comfy spots Timothy said "But yeah, when I told that nigga that, he knew without a doubt the kind of love I was talking about, and that's what triggered him when he came at me. I suppose he thought he was dealing with Timothy the church mouse, which was his first mistake. The second was when he had assumed I was weak because I was always in my bible and books, but I showed him otherwise. And he had best be glad yo brother told his boys to man down that day you called yo self-having a meeting with him".

Timothy had started playing a game on his phone as he spoke to me. I guess our kiss and the truth in my eyes were too much for him to bear so he'd picked it up after throwing me his Mentos, but after he said that, he looked up as if he'd said too much.

I was about to start asking a thousand questions when he said "Joanna" then gave me a look that said *if you wanna her the rest you bet not,* so I closed my mouth thinking *this is so not fair!* And so he continued "He came at me and it was on from there. I don't know why these cocky niggas think somebody's gonna be intimidated by them because they got a couple of muscles, but I showed his ass. But anyway, I gave him a run for his money, and with every punch, I made sure he felt the passion of my love for you." He looked at me out of the corner of his eyes when he said that but I didn't flinch, I needed to know what the hell went down.

I was starting to get real impatient but held my peace and that's when he said "I don't know how it happened, but somehow one of my Tim's came off, and while we were tussling I stepped on it and lost my footing. My back landed on the balcony rail and that's when his punk ass went in for the kill, otherwise his ass was grass. With his arms wrapped around my legs I heard him say 'Tell her muthafuckun broth'. Timothy caught himself, and stopped again. I was on the edge of my seat waiting on him to say more, but instead he said "That's it." I hopped up off his bed and screamed "WHAT!? What the heck you mean that's it? What did Rufus tell you to tell my brother Timothy? Huh? Why won't ya'll tell me nothin'? So did you tell'em? Did you tell Jonathan what Rufus wanted him to know"? Timothy looked at me with a confused look on his face and said "Jonathan? He didn't want me to tell Jonathan a damn thang, he was talking about Jude."

I sat down on his bed with my mouth wide open. *Jude? Why would Rufus want Timothy to give Jude a message?* Timothy looked at me like *aww shit, I dun messed up.* I didn't even care. All that Timothy had told me had me so confused I found myself getting a headache.

I laid down on his bed flat on my back and put my arm over my eyes. Timothy was stiff as a board and quietly asked "Joanna?" I held my other hand up and said "No more Timothy, I can't take anymore tonight" and that's when I felt him sit back and relax. I could feel him staring at me, but I didn't budge. *What in the hell was going on with Rufus and my brothers? And why was everybody keeping everything from me, like it's a big damn secret!*

I felt Timothy wiping a tear off the side of my face. I hadn't even realized that I had been crying. With my arm still over my eyes, I took my other hand and grabbed his. I kissed it and said "It's ok Timothy, I know ya'll are just trying to protect me. But how do ya'll expect me to win if I don't know what I'm fighting against?" Timothy pulled me up into a sitting position and as he did I thought *dang he strong.* He pulled me close, looked me eye to eye and then said "Joanna honey, you don't know what kind of force you're dealing with. They call that nigga Ruthless Rufus out on the streets and they don't call him that for nothing. What he tried to force you to do in that hotel room". My eyes got bigger than a mug! *How in the hell Timothy know about what Rufus did to me in that hotel, he don't even live in my state!* Timothy got a little frustrated with me, like my naiveness was wearing thin on him. With a frown on his face he said "Hell Joanna, everybody knows about what he did to you. Rufus's ass loves to brag, thinks it makes him look like a big man, but Jude put his foot in that ass". My eyes got big again. *Jude!? Not my Jude! But my big brother is so sweet and quiet. And always up in the church.* I guess what they say is true, it's the quiet ones you gotta look out for. As he beheld the confused look on my face, he

74

in return gave me a look like fuck it and told me so much stuff about my brothers, I didn't leave his room till after midnight.

I drove home in a daze. All this time I've been thinking Jonathan wasn't to be played with when in actuality it was Jude. Timothy told me that from the time of the skating rink incident to now, Jude had been kicking Rufus's ass every time he got a chance. I could not wrap my mind around that. *Jude? My sweet loving Jude?* I knew he had a temper, but I didn't know it was that bad, and then it hit me. My brothers were the way they were because of me, well Jude anyway because Jonathan had always been a roughneck sneaky butt. I had seen Jude act a fool maybe once or twice, and when he did, the world had best be aware because he clowned! Were my choices towards Rufus causing Jude to birth the monster he tries so hard to suppress? Dang that was deep! It was so deep that as I walked into the house I barely heard Faith as she excitedly said "Joanna girl, look what my friend got me". I looked down at the Louis Vuitton wallet she held towards me and unintentionally burst her bubble when I said "Girl that's a knockoff" and then went into my room.

Chapter Five

~Rufus~

I told you not to fuck with me Juicy, now I got sumthin' fo dat azz...

I had made the dean's list, again. Whoot~Whoot! Because I was constantly making good grades, the school started offering me scholarships which lessened my out of pocket expenses, and allowed me to save a few coins. On a humble, I decided to splurge and get myself a new comforter. I was real picky when it came to my purchases and made sure I got the best deal for my dollar. When I saw a black and turquoise comforter that had pretty silver crosses throughout it I thought *I bet daddy would pick this one out for me and bought it.* I couldn't wait to put it on my bed so that I could take a picture of it and send it to my parents.

When I walked into the house, Faith was sitting on the couch flicking through channels. Although my arms were full, she jumped up really fast to show me a bracelet a friend of hers had gotten her. It was kinda irritating because my arms were full with my packages, until her bling dang near blinded me.

I dropped my comforter and grabbed her wrist. I sang "Daaang girl! That has gots ta be at least a carat or one in a half. Who dropped those jewels on you"? I looked up into my friends eyes and saw them shining just as bright as her bracelet and was truly happy for her.

Faith had been through the ringer with those college boys. Of course she was boy crazy, and could have had dang near any boy she wanted, that's just how pretty she was. But time and time again she ended up with a broken heart because she refused to give up the goods. We had stayed up many a nights talking about the situations she always found herself in, and because of my one and only traumatic experience with Rufus, one I didn't tell her about, I encouraged her to stick to her guns and to not relent, no matter how hard it was. Then the guys started buying her gifts, and most were cheap and trashy but this! Now this was a gift.

Just when I was about to ask her about the mystery man, there was a knock at the door. When I opened it there was a UPS man standing with a package. He said it was for me and as I signed the paperwork, I had a surprised look on my face like *for me? Who in the world was sending me a gift?* And then I got excited, thinking it was from either Jonathan or Jude. It had been a while since I'd gotten anything from them, so when the UPS man left,

Faith and I were super hyped, and her bracelet was a forgotten thought.

The box was big but light, which made it hard to guess what was inside. I asked Faith to get a knife, and when she brought it back, I carefully cut the box opened. After removing the paper that was securing its content, I looked into the box and started rolling on the floor laughing. Faith looked at me like I was crazy, and when I could get my breath I told her to open the bag that I had brought in. When she took out my comforter, and looked at the one sticking out of the box, she started cracking up too. I guess great minds think alike because as I read the card that came with the comforter it said "Your daddy saw this at the store, and fell in love with it, so he decided to send it to you", and at the bottom she'd written "Love mommy and daddy". It was exactly the same comforter I'd just purchased. I absolutely loved my parents!

****

It was fall break, and although Timothy was walking, it was with a cane so instead of going home, I decided to hang out with my bud. He had told me numerous times that he would be ok, but when I flat out informed him that I wasn't going anywhere, I could tell he was grateful. After a quick visit, I decided to head to the house earlier than usual. For some reason I was tired and wanted to hit the sack so that I could rest my sluggish body. I said my goodbyes to Timothy and made it home in no time.

When I walked in I noticed a jacket laid across the arm of the couch. Out of habit I picked it up and hung it in the entryway closet. I took off my own jacket and hung it up as well. I grabbed a bottle of water out of the fridge then headed to my room. As I walked past Faith's door I heard what I thought were moaning sounds. In my mind I thought *naw, it couldn't be, not Faith?* But to be sure, I put my ear up to her door. I still couldn't make out the sound, so I quietly cracked it opened, just enough to sneak a peek. When my eyes adjusted to the light, I saw Faith laid on her back with eyes closed and her legs up. I looked at the guy between them, and my eyes met the eyes of Rufus's. He lifted his head, licked his lips, gave me an evil smile, blew me a kiss, and with his eyes still on me, commenced to finish eating my roommate's pussy.

My heart started beating fast as I closed the door just as quietly as I had opened it. I then went into my room, closed and locked my door. I laid on my back looking at the ceiling and thought *now it all makes sense.*

The first gift Rufus had gotten Faith was a knockoff Louis Vuitton wallet. He knew I knew real when I saw it, so when she went to him about what I said, he knew I was paying attention, but then he switched it up to try to confuse me. Instead of getting her everything Louis Vuitton, he went Coach. Coach shoes, bags, wallets, watches, and book bags. Coach everything. When I had come home with the comforter, my admiration of the bracelet was cut short by the doorbell, but over days, weeks and months, the gifts were getting more and more expensive.

At times I would ask Faith who the mystery guy was, but she said she was sworn to secrecy, and that she wouldn't tell because he didn't want anyone to know. I always gave her a sideways glance when she said that, because it was hard to believe a dude really didn't want anybody knowing he was feeling one of the most sought after girls on campus. A couple of times I would press her to see if she would break, and right before she'd start to whisper his name, I'd tell her she was good, because I didn't want her messing up a good thing because of my longing to know. She would always get a look of relief on her face when I said that and then continue to tell me how awesome her new friend was.

As I lay in my bed I thought of my friend *poor Faith, he's just using you to get to me.* She was really caught up too, and had fallen for the same tactic I had, stuff. But as I laid in my bed, I found myself putting a pillow between my legs, because the louder Faith moaned, the more my pussy jumped.

I was getting sexually frustrated when at an inopportune time I heard my phone vibrate. With major tude, I snatched it off the nightstand and read "I've missed you Juicy" just as I heard Faith cry out in ecstasy.

Chapter Six

~Rufus~

Time to come home Juicy. It's time to come home.

I mentioned nothing about what I'd seen or heard to Faith, and went about my daily routine as if I wasn't affected, but I was. *My freaking flesh!* I had never touched myself, but that visual of Rufus between Faith's legs caused the flame I thought I'd blown out, to be rekindled. Late at night I would wake up on fire. I wouldn't be thinking about anything before I'd go to sleep but Jesus, but then Rufus and his touch would invade my dreams. I would ease my hand between my legs trying to suppress my longing for his touch, but would only end up more agitated.

Rufus switched it up again. He had gotten Faith the exact same gifts he'd gotten me, the items were exactly identical, and Louis Vuitton. She would bounce into the house ecstatic about what her boo thang had gotten her. I would have to fake excitement, knowing I had given the same crap to my Aunt and cousins. It was actually pretty sad because Faith was falling in love with the devil, the same way I had thought I had. She would always ask me for relationship advice and I would tell her the same thing I had told her before I knew Rufus was the mystery man, to keep all her cookies in the cookie jar until her wedding night. While telling her these things, I could tell she wasn't really listening. She would always have a faraway look on her face, like she was thinking about the next gift he was going to surprise her with. Once she snapped out of her trek down the road of accumulation, she'd give me her undivided attention with her eyes aglow. I finally stopped answering her questions because for some reason, I knew it was just a matter of time before she fell into Rufus's spell.

I didn't call Rufus the devil for nothing. That boy was sneaky and slick when it came to using crafty tactics to pull my attention off Christ, and into his inferno. I remember, just like it was yesterday, when Faith had rushed into the house jumping up and down in excitement over a new gift. She was so excited that she ignored the fact that I was studying for the three exams that I had the following day. The whole week she had been quiet as a church mouse and had chosen the day before my exams to act a fool. I looked up from my laptop like *I know she did not just mess up my vibe.* But Faith was in Faith's world and hadn't even noticed the scrawl on my face. She was clueless so I figured I would use that moment to take a break. My head was starting to hurt and besides that, I was hungry.

I placed my laptop to the side and said "What's up my friend, ya mystery man trying to purchase ya with another gift?" I regretted saying those words as soon as they floated out of my mouth. I looked up at Faith, ready to apologize, but I didn't need too because she hadn't even noticed the shade I had thrown her way. I got up off the couch, thankful she hadn't, because although she was being used and taken advantage of without her knowledge, she was still my girl. I wanted to hip her up about Rufus so bad I could taste it, but by the time I had found out who the mystery man was, she was already caught up. I knew she wouldn't see my informing her as a blessing in disguise, but rather as jealousy.

As I walked into the kitchen, Faith was dead on my heels, and when I had turned around to get some bread, I ran smack dead into her, which caused us both to laugh. I knew she was bubbling over with excitement to show me her new prize, but my stomach was on "e" for empty and needed immediate attention. She got the hint and went and sat at the dining room table and started shaking her leg because she could barely hold what she wanted to tell me much longer.

After fixing my food and saying my grace, I took a big bite of my sandwich and said, "Fuz zp grl" with a mouth full of food. No interpretation was needed as she put her hands on the side of her face and asked, with big bright eyes "You notice anything different?" While chewing and squinting, I started looking at her real intently, and nothing looked different to me. I then looked at her eyelashes thinking that maybe she had finally done what she had been contemplating doing, and had gotten her first set of fake ones, but nope, all I saw was Faith. She started wiggling her fingers, and that's when I saw the huge piece of bling on her right hand. I hopped up outta my chair and ran to her side. I grabbed her hand and yelled "Holy shit!" I put my hand over my mouth and said "My bad girl, but this ring is freaking breathtaking". I stared down at that ice cold rock in awe, and although I hated myself for this, I felt a sting of jealousy. That ring was absolutely gorgeous. I held her hand in mine as she went on and on about how he had surprised her after one of her classes.

****

She said that as she walked out of her class door, she felt her phone vibrate and when she had a moment she pulled it out and noticed that her mystery man had text "What's that in your book bag?" She said she didn't have a clue as to what he was talking about so she went to the nearest bench to find out. After sitting down she started digging deep within her bag. When nothing looked amiss she dug deeper. She said she began to get frustrated because after she had taken everything out, and still hadn't found anything. On a humble she turned her bag upside down and started shaking all the scraps of paper and crumbs out, and that's when the surprise tumbled to the ground. She said that it had been hard to find because somehow Rufus had cut a little slit in the bottom of her book bag, and had tucked the ring deep within its pocket.

Because she wasn't expecting it to be a ring she looked at it in total shock as it lay on the ground, wrapped in a pretty silver box. She said she slowly picked it up and then opened it. Her hand flew to her chest because she could not believe her eyes as her mouth dropped open wide enough to host a colony of flies. With shaking hands, she put the ring on her finger, and then turned her hand in every direction, watching as the rays of sun pulled out its exquisite gracefulness.

While watching Faiths lips move I puld to help but think *he sure is digging deep to make me jealous,* and as she went on and on about the whole incident, I began to give her my undivided attention, because I knew, without a doubt, that her happiness would be short lived.

****

Later that evening Faith and her mystery man had plans to go to dinner. When she told me that, I retired earlier than usual to my bedroom. I realized I did not want to be in the same proximity as Rufus, not even for the few seconds it would take for him to pick her up. After they'd left, I decided to stay in my room because my brain was fried, so after saying my prayers, I officially turned out the lights at midnight.

I was in a good, deep, sleep when at about two o'clock in the morning I felt pressure at the end of my bed, but thought I was dreaming. I felt a soft kiss on my inner thigh, then a finger pulling my panties to the side. I could feel his hot breath over my pearl and then his tongue. That's when I knew I wasn't dreaming. I didn't open my eyes, and as Rufus went to town, I opened my legs wider and put both my hands on top of his head. I started rolling my hips and tried hard to suppress my moans. It felt so damn good! I grabbed my pillow and put it over my face because I knew it wouldn't be long before he took me there.

Rufus was not to be rushed and took his time, basking in my scent and sweetness. I heard him whisper "I've missed you Juicy, especially your taste". In my mind I thought *you miss my cousin too?* And although I wanted so bad for him to stop, I also wanted him to eat me like a starved animal walking in the desert in temps of over a hundred degrees longing for a drop, not a fountain, just a drop of water to quench his thirst. I started moaning into the pillow as Rufus sucked on my pearl. *I hate you Rufus!* I arched my back. He blew on my pearl. *I fucking hate you Rufus!* I rolled my hips. Rufus nibbled on my pearl. *I HATE YOU RUFUS!!!* I grip his neck with my knees, and squeeze. He softly bit my pearl. *I! FUCKING! HATE! YOU! RUFUS!* I push the pillow into my face. *YEEEEEEESSSSS! He* drinks from my fountain, and drinks from my fountain, and drinks from my fountain.

Rufus licked me dry, and then kissed me on my inner thighs, then down my legs, then my ankles, then took my toes into his mouth. I started getting aroused again. He said "I'm sorry I hurt you Juicy", then kissed the bottom of my feet, "I really do love you", then massaged my heels, "I've missed you like I would miss air if I had no life in me" and then he got up.

With the pillow still over my face, I knew Rufus had walked to my door. Before he opened it he said "I left you something" and then walked out.

pI laid there and cried. How in the world could I have let what just happened, happen!? Why didn't I stop him?! I knew what he was up too, I had known all along so why didn't I scream out to alert Faith, or tell him to leave me the hell alone? I hate when people ask me questions they already knew the answers to, and just like them, I knew the answer to my own damn question. I didn't do any of those things because I loved him.

I stayed in my bed for a few more minutes, then threw back my blanket so that I could go to the bathroom. When I made that move I heard something hit the wall then floor. *What in the world was that?* I closed my eyes and exhaled deeply. *Here we go again. He said he had left me something and I'm sure that something is what just flew across the room.* I turned on my bedroom light, and when I sat up I could still feel his presence all around me. I took in a long deep sniff. *Aww, his cologne,* and it smelled hella good. I looked in the direction of where I'd heard the sound of my "something" hitting the wall and saw a little silver box on the floor next to my bedroom door. I just shook my head and thought *that boy is a piece of work and bold as hell.*

I got up and walked over to pick it up, and as I was bending down I heard whispered giggles and voices outside my door. I felt bad as hell! I picked up the box and got back in the bed and under my covers. I'd already known what was inside because Faith had shown me hers a few hours earlier. I contemplated just throwing it in the trash, but thought better of it. I tossed the box back and forth between my hands going over in my mind what had just transpired, and then I stopped. I would have to think about that later, I had exams in a few hours and didn't want to even go there in my mind about anything concerning Rufus and his manipulative ways. Instead, I took that little box and angrily threw it up against the wall. *SHIT! SHIT! SHIT! Why do I keep letting that boy get under my skin?!*

As the box broke apart, the ring floated in the air like a magic spell and then hit the floor directly between my house shoes that were next to my bed. I reached down and picked it up. When my eye looked upon that ring my eyes got so huge, I felt my pupils dilate. *OH! MY! GOD!!!* I sat all the way erect and scooted closer to my lamp that was on my nightstand and that's when my damn hands started to shake. *OH! MY! GOD!!!* I looked on the inside of the ring to see what the carat was, and saw an inscription that read "I love you Joanna", then sat back in awe.

My mind was in a billion places at one time. Had Rufus really gotten this for me? I wasn't no jeweler, but I knew that ring had to have cost Rufus a grip. In the thousands kinda grip. My hands were still shaking as I got up enough courage to place it on one of my fingers. I held my hand up to the light and was at a loss for words. In actuality none were needed because the ring spoke volumes within itself.

I took the ring off and put it back into the portion of box that was still intact, that had landed near my nightstand. I then climbed outta bed, went to my closet and found an old, raggedy, shoebox. I dumped the contents to the floor, tore some notebook paper out my notebook, and securely wrapped it with about five sheets. I then put the contents back inside and put the shoebox in the very back of my closet, and covered it with clothes. I sat back on my hunches. *Yeah, Rufus had gotten Faith and I the exact same ring, but what I had held in my hand made Faith's ring look like it had come from a gum ball machine.* I got up, climbed back into bed, and pulled the covers up to my chin. I turned out the light with my eyes wide open, and laid in that position until the sun came up.

****

About a month had passed and I hadn't seen Rufus since the bedroom incident, which was fine by me. I had somewhat gotten my hormones under control, suppressing the urge to think on the night Rufus had taken me to ecstasy. And although I continued with my everyday routines, I would soon learn that Rufus's presence, and the lack thereof, had caused a shift in me that I hadn't even felt within myself.

It was during my visit with Timothy. I guess I was there and not there at the same time because out the blue he asked "How ya classes going?" I suppose I was having a "Not there" moment because I hadn't heard a word he'd said. He slapped my thigh and summoned me back to reality. Clueless I asked "What?" Timothy laughed and started snapping his fingers in front of my face saying "Earth to Joanna, earth to Joanna". In irritation I push his hand out of my face which caused him to give me a sideways glance. I turned my head away and continued to look at nothing as Timothy took his index finger and turned my head back in his direction. I abruptly stood up to leave.

As I was making a beeline to his door he grabbed me by my arm and said "Hey, hey, heeey. What is going on with you?" I flopped back down on his bed and told him "I'm good" with my eyes averted. Timothy wasn't buying it. He knew me like a book and wasn't accepting my lame excuse. He placed his hand on my knee, and for some reason that irritated me. I moved his hand on the sly, faking a stretch, while looking away. That boy didn't let nothing get passed him so he did it again and I responded the same way. With a soft gentle voice he asked "So what you been up too lady? You don't come through the way you used too". I turned my head in my friend's direction and all my tension left my body. In my mind I thought *if only you knew about my battle within* but said "You know finals are coming up soon. I been studying". Timothy cut me off by saying "Finals never stopped you before". He was right, whether rain, sleet or snow; nothing prohibited me from seeing my friend. I looked at the love and concern on his face and gave a little smile. I leaned in, gave him a kiss on the cheek and said "I've just been tired my man, no worries". Timothy took my hand and kissed my palm. He looked at me with the purest of hearts and said "I hope not".

Chapter Seven

~Rufus~

I promise to be gentle...

My flesh was getting the best of me, both physically and mentally. At night I would find myself staring at my closet door and when I could take it no more, I'd go to it, dig the shoebox from behind the millions of things I used to hide it from myself, and slowly open the jewelry box. I would sit on my floor and rub my index finger over the ring numerous times, drinking in its beauty.

One night, as I was doing that very thing, I heard light tapping outside my window. That sound scared me so bad I crawled into my closet. *What in the world are you doing Joanna?* As I crawled out I heard the tapping again. I slowly covered the ring back into the notebook paper, put it back in its box, pushed it deep into its home and then covered it back up with the junk I used to protect it. I got up off the floor and walked to my window. I didn't open it, I just stood there having an all-out battle with my flesh and spirit. I knew who was on the other side, it wasn't rocket science and although I hadn't seen nor talked to Rufus in weeks, he always found a way to force his way into my space.

My mind took me to the last lick down session he'd given me and I found myself squeezing my thighs together. In my mind I'd convinced myself that one last time wouldn't hurt nobody and pulled my curtain to the side then unlocked my window. I turned my lights out so that no one would see him come in but mostly because I didn't want to see him come in. No words were needed as Rufus slithered his way into my den of sin.

I saw his silhouette pick itself up off my floor and I ran into his arms. We both turned our heads to the side as our lips hungrily engulfed the others. Our hands were all over the place as we became re-familiar with each other once again. His big hands squeezed my butt real hard pushing me into his long hard log. I let off a soft moan when he placed it on my pearl. My moan set Rufus into a frantic frenzy as he took his mouth off mine and started sucking on my neck. That move made me weak at the knees. Rufus walked me backwards to the wall behind me, and once my back hit its surface he lifted me up so that I could wrap my legs around his waist. While sucking and licking on my neck he rolled my hips in a circular motion with his hardness against my pearl. When I started moaning too loud he put his hand over my mouth. As he put my legs down he whispered "Be quite Juicy" and then snatched off my shirt and lifted my bra off in one swoop and then started sucking on my breast.

Rufus started squeezing and sloppily licking and touching all over my body. While sucking on my right breast, he started sliding my pants and panties down but had trouble because they were still fastened and wouldn't budge over my wide hips. I started wiggling trying to help the process and when that didn't work, I removed my hands from around his waist and expedited the process by unbuttoning my pants and letting them drop to my ankles. I barely had one leg out when Rufus got to his knees, and put both my legs over his shoulders. I was waiting for the onslaught of his lips and tongue but it didn't come, instead he just sniffed. I started rolling my hips trying to force his mouth onto my flower. Rufus wasn't having that and said, louder than he should have, "Cut that shit out Juicy". I thought *fuck you Rufus!* And pushed his head towards my music box. He tried pulling his head back but because of his position he had no leverage. I was on fire and not getting the full force of what I knew Rufus had to offer because he was still trying to control how he was going to pleasure me, which pissed me off. I started acting like I was on a swing set and stretched my legs out, then brought them back while at the same time pushed my back and arms off the wall which caused Rufus to tumble backwards and land on his back with my pearl right where I wanted it, over his mouth.

I flipped my legs around and used them to pin his arms to the floor as I place my hands above his head and start grinding my stuff on his oral cave. I roll my hips with my head thrown back and my eyes closed real tight. Rufus freed his arms and wrapped them around my thighs and pulled me further down. That nigga act like he was eating some damn fried chicken as I felt his lips, teeth and tongue lick me from one hole to the other. As I rocked back and forth I started biting the inside of my mouth to keep from crying out. Rufus took one of his hands and unzipped his pants. As I continued to rock I could feel Rufus's shoulder muscle moving as he jacked himself off. When I realized what he was doing I got so turned on, I started tasting blood because I was biting my inner mouth so hard. I heard Rufus grunt which caused my magic box to vibrate and tip me over the edge. I pushed down so hard on Rufus's face, I wouldn't have been surprised if his ass had been dead after that lick session. I felt the pace of Rufus's muscle movement's increase, and as it increased, so did my hip motion. I don't know why but I kept asking myself stupid questions like *I wonder if he ate my cousin out?* His muscles moved faster and as they did, so did my hips and I thought *who does their baby look like? Him or her?* Rufus grunts and I feel his muscles slam straight to high speed jack off mode as I asked myself *I wonder how many times they fucked!?* Feeling that muscle accelerate under my ass caused me to arch my back, pull my blanket off my bed and smother my face in it. Rufus started breathing fast, as well as I. He's still stroking and I'm still rolling *he's gon pay for that shit!* He's still stroking and I'm still rolling *my damn cousin Rufus!* We grunt together as his body stiffens. I feel his seed squirt onto my back and think *what just hit my back was squirted into my cousins pussy.* I'm rolling my hips, *ima make you suffer for this shit Rufus!* I'm rolling my hips "You want me Rufus?" I'm rolling my hips "You! Mmmm, want! Mmm, me! Yessss, nigga!?" I'm rolling my hips "I'm about to make you wish you never met me". I stop rolling my hips and scream "Yes! Yes! Yes! Yeeeeeees!" into my blanket.

I climbed off Rufus's face and onto my floor. My heart was beating so fast I thought it was gonna jump out my chest. I was on my stomach when I felt Rufus start from the sole of my feet and kiss his way up to the back of my neck. His full lips felt so good, I started getting caught up again. I felt him place his hard log between my butt cheeks and start rolling his hips. I shut that dick action down real quick and told him "I think it's time for you to go" as I flipped onto my back. In a high pitched voice Rufus said "Huh?" I repeated myself "I think it's time for you to go". Rufus bent his head down and started placing soft kisses on my neck, I politely gave him a little shove up off me and although it was pitch black in my room, I hopped up with my blanket wrapped around my body, then pointed to the window. I couldn't see Rufus, but I could feel his emotions through that

Angela Moore

thick fog of darkness, and he was not a happy camper, but I didn't give a damn.

As he got up, he started putting his goods back into his boxers. While quietly getting himself together, I could feel him smiling. He said "Oh, so you bad now huh?" I put my hand on my hip, tilted my head to the side and said "Bye Rufus". He stood there, with his hands in his pockets playing with his change, while rocking back and forth on his heels. He walked towards me and in a husky voice said "Juicy?" I half ran half walked to my door and with my hand on the knob said "I'll open it Rufus, I promise I will" to which he replied "I wish I gave a damn". I took my hand off the knob, walked up to him and through clenched teeth said "Just like I wish I didn't give a damn about you and my muthafuckun cousin! Now get the fuck up out my room you trifling bitch!" Rufus knew I was crying, even in the dark. He took a step towards me which caused my arm to automatically draw back and slap his ass so hard, the sensation traveled to my shoulder. We stood there in the dark listening to my weeping. How Faith slept through all that, I'll never know because a whole lot had went down in my room and none of it had been quiet. My pain was palpable, and when he could take it no more, he left exactly the same way he had come.

****

97

I was home for winter break and lord knows I needed it. Rufus had done another disappearing act, and had somehow convinced Faith to not mention anything about him while in my presence, which was fine by me. Those last few weeks of class were torture enough without the added stress of hearing about a relationship that was doomed from the start.

My visits with Timothy had spread out to almost nonexistent, although he continued to send me his verse of the day. I just didn't feel like being bothered. Hanging with Timothy may have helped me in many ways, especially in diverting my attention from negative energy to positive, but at the time, I wasn't trying to deal with nobody. That winter break couldn't have come soon enough.

I think going away to school allowed me to eventually mature a little bit. The whole Rufus incident hadn't consumed me the way it had previously done when he'd called me a bitch. His moves towards my roommate confirmed that he would go to extreme lengths to accomplish whatever he set out to do, even if it was something insane. And his warped mentality helped me place him in the proper compartment of my life which gave me a growth spurt into reality. It was still extremely hard for me to wrap my mind around him having a baby by my cousin, but once I started convincing myself that if I had no expectations of people, then there would be no disappointment, I began to accept people where they were. And that included Rufus. During that time, unbeknown to me, just as I had placed everybody on the same plain of pushing them out of my life, I had also, over time, pushed God out as well.

****

As an Adams family tradition, the entire Adams clan came together to celebrate Thanksgiving. It would be during the previous year's Thanksgiving feast that everyone would learn the name of the lucky family that would be hosting Thanksgiving feast in the year to come. To accomplish that feat, everyone's name, except the family that was hosting and the host family from the previous year, would be put into a hat. So no one would think the person who was pulling out the name was being shiesty, the adults would call one of the little kids into the adult circle and allow them to do the honor of pulling out a name. Aunt B and her crew were always invited, but never participated, until that year. And guess whose turn it was to host the festivities for the entire family the year she decided to participate? None other than ours.

It felt so good to be home, and although Jonathan and Jude were out living on their own, they were at the house whenever they had some free time. I was in nirvana as my family doted on me and spoiled me rotten, just like old times. Mommy and I shopped for, and cooked the meats for the holiday, while all the other families were in charge of bring the sides. We made turkey, ham, Cornish hens and chitterlings. Daddy and his brothers were born and bred in the city but if you were to base their birthplace by their diet, you'd have thought they were all country boys. They loved country cooking so much, that one of the brothers opened a southern food Restaurant.

As with anything the Adam boys put into practice, the restaurant was used as a means of ministry to help out of work veterans make a decent and honest living, while also providing the ones who were homeless a warm and clean bed at night in the adjacent house that was directly in back of the restaurant. At times, family members would order their already assigned side dish from the restaurant which helped sustain the family owned business, while also relieving them from the task of slaving over the stove preparing food for so many people. I had been given the dutiful job of taking all foods that were brought over into the kitchen so that mama and the ladies could place them in there designated location. As I walked in with my favorite big cousins upside down cake, I overheard my mom say "Really? Praise The Lord!" While lifting her hands above her head. Of course I had to find out what that was about, so I asked "What are you getting all excited and praising The Lord for now mommy?" and before I could hand the cake I was carrying over to one of my Aunts, my mama said "Because God is good! You're Aunt B and the kids are coming down for Thanksgiving this year" which caused my favorite big cousins upside down cake to end up just like its names sake, upside down, as I dropped it on the floor.

When I bent over to pick it up, I vomited, then started sweating profusely. My mom and Aunts rushed over to my side, asking if I was ok, which caused me to throw up again. One of my Aunts rushed into the bathroom to get me a cold face towel, because my entire body was hot. While she was doing that, mommy and my other Aunts walked me to my bedroom and assisted me in getting into my bed. I had my eyes closed when I felt the wonderful sensation of that coolness being placed on my forehead. I opened one eye and told my Aunts and mom that I was fine and that it was ok for them to finish up the cooking. They were real reluctant to leave until I persuaded them by letting them know that I was probably exhausted, and that I would be out to mingle with the family after I'd taken a nap. As they started making their exit, mommy lingered and placed her hand on my head making sure I didn't have a fever. I told her to stop fussing over me and that there were a whole lotta people trying to get fed and the head chef attending to her little girl wasn't a good enough excuse to make them wait any longer. With a worried look on her face, she gave me a kiss and left. I guess I really was exhausted because three hours later, I opened my eyes to see a miniature Rufus standing next to my bed, staring dead at me.

I turned my head and saw my cousin Tamar posted up in my bedroom door. With a smirk on her face, she had the nerve to sing "Wat up cuuuuuz?"

like all was well. I put my eyes on the boy and snapped when Tamar said "Bring yo ass over here R.J., you did good baby". I climbed out of my bed so fast I left my thoughts in the wind. I slapped baby Rufus so hard across the room, that by the time his mama realized what I'd done, he had landed face first at her feet. I grabbed her stank ass by her 2,000$ weave, which I'm sure Rufus paid for, and threw her to the floor. I started stomping her in her face and wherever my feet would land. I said absolutely nothing as all my rage was transferred from my heart to my feet, so no words were needed.

The next thing I knew I felt some big strong arms grip me around my waist and simultaneously lift me off my feet. As I was being twirled around, I saw my whole family in my doorway trying to get a peek at what was going on. Once I was able to have my brain catch up with my body, I looked down at my cousin on the floor, placed my hand over my opened mouth and said "I am sooo sorry cuz! I am so, so sorry! You cain't be sneaking up on me like that while I'm sleep" and started rubbing my eyes. I was slowly being placed back on my feet as everybody realized it was all a big mistake. I bent to my knees and stretched out my arms to a weeping Rufus Jr. telling him "Tuuuum mere lil man." He held on to his mama's leg for dear life as Jude helped her up off the floor. Where my calmness and that lie came from, who knows, but it was right on time.

I stood up with a pure and innocent look on my face as I asked someone to bring me a face towel so that I could wipe off the blood that was pouring out of Tamar's nose. When I said that she looked at me like *Bitch! You got me fuuucked up!* While making a quick exit out of my bedroom door. Jude started helping me pick up items that had fallen during the ruckus. Mama brought me some soap and water in a bucket so I began the task of scrubbing Tamar's blood off my floor. While on my hands and knees I saw Jonathan's shoes in my bedroom door, and when I looked up, I noticed he had a smirk on his face. As he looked down on me, he took a sip of the pop that was in his hand, and then turned to go finish his meal.

Cleaning up that mess wore me out and made me funky so I took a shower then made my way out to chill with my family. Aunt B and her crew had left by then, but I didn't care, I was over it. Seeing R.J. had tipped me over the edge. Rufus telling me that Tamar was the mother of his child was one thing; her flaunting that shit in my face was another. It also confirmed my deepest fear, which caused me to just not give a damn anymore.

While trying to have a decent time with my family, everything I had been thru with Rufus kept replaying itself in my mind. After I had gotten one of my uncle's a piece of pie, I changed one of my younger cousin's diaper, and then helped the ladies clean up the kitchen. As I did all of that my mind played a movie that consisted of constant pain and turmoil, with very few moments of joy. I promised myself that I was going to make Rufus pay for his bold display of disrespect. For causing me to be the laughing stock of the hood and probably the campus as well. For being that boil, that no matter how many times I squeezed, always came back. For making me fall in love with him and for every bruise to my heart that he had inflicted. Yeah, Rufus was about to pay, starting that night.

Chapter Eight

~Rufus~

Juicy. Oh Juicy, Juicy, Juicy, you   are no match for me my dear!

The house was quiet and thank God Jonathan and Jude had decided to go hang with other family members instead of staying the night at the house. I had text Rufus earlier in the day to let him know that I wanted to talk to him, and of course, he agreed. I had to make sure my parents were out for the count, so it was after one in the morning when I was able to get away. We kept the meeting place simple, the school park.

Rufus had the car running and warm when I got in. No words were spoken as he drove me to the most   expensive   luxury   hotel   in   downtown Indianapolis. When we pulled up I immediately thought *wonder if he brought that trick cousin of mine up here,* but shifted gears because I was on a mission. Rufus gave his car keys to the valet but opened my door himself. We walked in not saying anything as he led the way into the room. Of course it was exquisite, but I paid no attention to that, as I had one thing on my mind.

I went straight to the bathroom and took a shower. As I came out, he walked in. I was in the bed under the blankets when Rufus exited, wet with a towel around his waist. He dropped it and was standing at attention as he climbed into the bed next to me. He started kissing, and touching me with a passion I had never experienced before. I was stiff as a stone, just like his dick. Rufus paid me no mind as he pulled back the blanket, admiring my body. In a hoarse voice he said "Damn you're beautiful" while stroking my breast. It hit him that I wasn't responding to his touch so he stopped. He got a smirk on his face and grabbed my ankles, pulling me close to him. He placed my legs over his shoulders as he bent down and took a sniff of my music box. Our eyes were locked on each other's as he took his fingers and opened me wide. While looking at me he slowly started playing a score with his tongue but no music was heard. He added suction to my needle, with no reaction from me. He started licking, which rendered the same response, which pissed him off. He licked me from top to bottom, nothing. He sucked my toes, legs, knees and thighs, nothing. He angrily yanked me by my ankles again, placed my legs on either side of his waist then leaned down towards me placing his hands on either side of my head, with our eyes still on lock. He hit the mattress with such force, I thought I felt heat pass my face. I didn't budge. He said "What the fuck you want from me Juicy? Huh? I already told yo ass that I was sorry, so now what?" I said nothing. He started getting angrier, but then changed tactics by saying "Look Juicy, I'm sorry baby, I really am, and I'll do whatever it takes to make it up to you, anything." I said "Anything?" And with a satisfied smile on his face he said "Yeah baby, anything you want, I'll do it." I asked "Where's your phone?"

Rufus sat up when I asked that, and with a frown on his face asked "What the fuck you need my phone for?" I said nothing and waited for fifteen minutes as he had a battle within trying to figure out my angle, and when I didn't relent, he reached down into his pants and brought it out. While holding it between his thumb and index finger he twirled it back and forth and then asked "Now what?" Through clenched teeth I said "Now what? Now you call that nasty trick hoe ass cousin of mine, and tell that bitch that as of right now, you won't be doing shit for nobody up in that house but your son". Rufus looked at me like I was crazy, face all ugly and everything. He said "Wa? Is that all you won't?" then called her phone. I was about to say "And put that shit on speaker phone too", but before I could, I realized he had already done it when I heard my cousin say "Wats up Ru? I miss you baby. You check that bitch about our son yet?" Rufus held up a finger in my direction when he saw me raising up, about to speak and said "Look here, watch ya mouth cause I'm calling to check yo azz, so looka here. It's over, everything is over. I'll be through to touch base with my son and that's all I'll be touchin'. Keep ya palms in ya pockets because from now on, I'll be haven my mama get errthing R.J. needs" click!

Rufus looked down at me like he'd done something good, but instead of giving him a smile, I opened up my legs. With a smile on his face he asked "Oh, so it's like that huh?".

As he started kissing my neck, my breast and licked my collarbone, Rufus said "Look at me Juicy" so I did. I leaned up on my elbows and watched as Rufus licked and kissed my whole body. While looking at me, he used his fingers to open me wide. He brought his nose close, sniffed really deep, and then closed his eyes. He swallowed hard as his mouth started watering, and just before he was about to get it in, with his eyes locked on mine he said "Juicy, don't you ever put yo muthafuckun hands on my son again, and if you do, ima break them bitches" and then proceeded to licked my needle.

Angela Moore

Chapter Nine

~Rufus~

Ahhh, looks like we've got company.

Rufus drove me to the same spot he had picked me up. It was four o'clock in the morning, and I was tired. Rufus and I hadn't had sex, but he had given me a nice long lick session that produced three hard orgasms. On the ride to the park, Rufus had one of his underground rap CDs playing, and it was giving me a headache. I had my head leaned back on the headrest with my eyes closed, but sat up and opened them when I felt the car slowing down. Although the park was dark, I was able to see the shadows of two people playing basketball when Rufus's lights had shined on them as we had turned the corner. *What idiots are playing ball at this hour?* After Rufus had parked and hit the lights, I watched as the shadows started walking in our direction. With his eyes on those two, Rufus leaned close to me and said "Give me a kiss Juicy". I totally ignored him as my eyes adjusted to the guy who was holding the basketball under his arm, Jude, and his partner in crime, my big brother Jonathan.

I lowered my head and shook it back and forth. *Oh shit!* I know I should have known better, but I was so angry and caught up with making Rufus pay and him putting Tamar in check, that I had been negligent. Oh well, it was time for me to face the music.

Rufus lowered the volume on his radio, and then rolled his windows down. Jude was leaning into my window while Jonathan was in Rufus's. They both said "Wazup Ru" at the same time, and I almost pissed my pants. Rufus said "Wazup Adam boys" with such an arrogant tone; I lifted my head and looked at him like he was crazy. Jude unlocked and opened my door and said "Go home Joanna", like the whole situation was nothing. Like it was something as simple as him catching me taking the long route home from the candy store, instead of the route mama had told me to take.

I did not want to get out that car. I hadn't forgotten what Timothy had told me about Jude, and although I had come up with my own plan to pay Rufus back for what he had done to me, my plan did not include my brothers. I looked up at Jude, and neither one of us had an expression on our face. In his calm, soothing voice he said "Don't make me repeat myself". I got out, kissed him on his face, and with my head down, started walking home. When I heard two car doors close, I turned around and watched as Rufus drove off with my brothers in tow.

110

About a month later I took notice of a long scar going down the side of Jonathan's face. After that night, he had disappeared just as Rufus had. Mommy and daddy had tried to coax him to all the holiday excitement, but he pleaded work every time. Jude on the other hand didn't miss a beat, nor a free meal, as he made sure he was in attendance of them all. During the New Year celebration at church, Jude and I were reaching for the same piece of pie when I saw a blood soaked gauze creeping from under the wrist part of his jacket. My eyes got big as the pie as I squeaked out "What the hell?" He looked down and saw what I saw, and that's when we both noticed that blood was seeping through the underarm portion of his jacket itself. He hurriedly put his arm down and made a quick exit with me right on his heels. He got into his car and so did I. He told me to get out but I wasn't budging. He started his ride and drove us to mommy and daddy's house.

As I unlocked the front door, he popped his trunk and brought out a huge Walmart bag. Once inside, we went directly to the bathroom. I helped my big brother take off his jacket and shirt, and then jumped back with my hand over my mouth, shocked at what I saw. I thought I was gonna be sick. Jude had a raw, infected, opened gash going from under his arm around to his forearm and it smelled horrible. I asked no questions about how he got it because I already knew, but what I did wanna know was why he hadn't gone to a doctor. I guess he could sense my fear, because as he took the blood soaked gauze off, and started preparing to redress his wound, he said that there was no way he could go to any bodies anything without mommy and daddy finding out.

He turned on the water and started cleaning the gash with a warm face towel. He then took out a jar of cream and placed some on the wound, and like a master surgeon he took some surgical tape and secured the gauze, which was soon re-soaked. With my hand still covering my nose, I picked up the container and asked what it was. With a proud look on his face he said "Something my ingenious mind put together", broke out into a sweat, then passed out.

I looked down at my brother super scared. *What the hell!?* As I reached down to check his pulse, the way I'd seen people do on TV, I called Jonathan in a panic, and before he could say hello I said "Jude's cheap butt dun passed out! He's on the floor at mommies. What do I do Jonathan? He said he didn't wanna go to the hospital because of some of the church members working there, what do I do? He's turning pale right before my eyes", and when I said that I burst into tears.

Jonathan talked to me as he drove to the house, but I didn't know that, and as I was screaming for him to get his ass there, I heard him behind me as he was hanging up his phone. I ran into his arms as he pushed me to the side and walked straight to Jude. *Well damn!* And that's when I noticed a group of guys behind him. They picked Jude up and started taking him to a car. Just as I hung my mouth wide opened, dumbfounded as I looked at the brother I hadn't see in over a month, mama called asking me where we were. I could not believe the gash that was on Jonathan's face! He still had freaking stitches in it! *Oh my goodness, what in the hell happened that night? And where in the hell is Rufus?* A cold chill engulfed me as I thought the worse. *Lord, please don't let them have killed Rufus! Oh my Lord! Oh my Lord!* Mommy's sharp tone brought me back to reality as I said, in a fake sick voice, "I think me and Jude might have food poisoning mommy. We been eating those Christmas leftovers and I think they got the best of us". As mommy scolded me and Jude for not being considerate enough to say bye, I stood in the front door and watched my brothers pull off going to who knows where.

Mommy was going on and on when my phone clicked. I saw that it was Jonathan and thought *I am not about to click over and give mommy a reason to start asking a thousand questions.* He blew my phone up! I finally said "Mommy, I think ima be sick" trying to get her off the phone. Wrong move. Immediately she wanted to leave the New Year's celebration to come home and attend to me. I rolled my eyes up in my head and told her that, that wasn't necessary and that I would take some Pepto-Bismol and lay down. As mommy continued to make sure I was ok, my phone beeped, letting me know I had a text. I put mommy on speaker and read *that had best to be somebody in the family you ignoring me for!!!* It was Jonathan, so when I read that, I text back *duh!*

And just as I had hit send, another text came in that said *bathroom.* I whispered "Shit!" as I ran into the kitchen for cleaning supplies, and then I heard mommy ask "What did you just say?"

Chapter Ten

~Rufus~

His ass got eyes everywhere, but you know what? So do I.

After winter break, mommy and daddy had to take me back to school. Both Jude and Jonathan were ghost, and no matter how hard my parents tried, they could not make them reappear. I don't know why my brothers kept so many things from me, I could only assume that they were trying to protect me from the dangers that really existed, but I couldn't see that far ahead.

Before I left to go back to school, I was blowing both Jude and Jonathan's phones up, but they'd never call back, they'd just *text we're good Ladybug,* which made me mad. On the drive to school, as I looked out the window, I replayed everything that happened over the break in my mind and came to the conclusion that it was all madness. How could one person invade dang near a whole family's psyche with their presence? Even while absent Rufus was in a room. I couldn't wrap my mind around that, and by the time we'd pulled up to my house, I had stopped trying too.

I text Jonathan and Jude to let them know we'd made it safely. Faith was already home when we pulled up and help unload all the gifts I had chosen to bring with me from mommy and daddy's. She said "Dang girl! It's like you moving in here for the first time with all this stuff you got". I guess I didn't realize how much I had until she'd mentioned it. Once everything was inside, I looked around my room and thought *dang, this is a lotta stuff,* as we started organizing and putting things away. When we were finished, mommy and daddy took us to a late dinner, which was right on time.

We decided on a small family owned restaurant that was located on campus. After placing our orders, we were chatting it up when I saw Timothy and his parents walk in. I hopped up out of my chair and ran into his arms. I kissed him all over his face as everybody watching started cracking up. I had really freaking missed my friend!!! Although his parents didn't want to intrude, I had insisted they eat with us, and just as they were sitting down, Rufus walked in on some crutches.

Faith made the same moves I'd made towards Timothy when Rufus walked through the door, and although her jumping into his arms caused him pain, he played it off like it was no big deal. She grabbed him by his hand and escorted him to our table. I immediately thought *awww shit!* As Rufus took a seat directly across from me. Faith took his crutches

116

and laid them quietly on the floor next to them, then made the introductions. Faith started cheesin' real hard when daddy said "Don't I know you? I never forget a face, don't tell me, don't tell me" while tapping his index finger on his lower lip. Mama rolled her eyes to the sky then started laughing along with Timothy's mom at my dad's dramatics. Daddy eventually told us all to carry on, and that when it came to him, he'd let us know.

Faith was sitting so close to Rufus, she left no space in between, and I could tell he was a little agitated. As Rufus looked at his menu, he acted as if Timothy and I didn't exist, but I could feel the fire of his temperament from across the table. I guess Timothy was going to take advantage of the opportunity that had presented itself and grind it into Rufus's face. When the waitress came over to take Rufus's drink order, Timothy scooted closer to me and asked the waitress "Could you hold on for a minute please ma'am" then looked down at me and asked "You want any desert baby?" I had to bite the inside of my mouth to keep from laughing. I picked up a menu then said "Hmmm, you know what? I think I do. You wanna share a piece of chocolate cake with me? Oh, and I wanna thank you again for my Christmas gift, you are the sweetest!" then gave him a kiss on the cheek. I heard daddy, all the way at the end of the table, clear his throat which caused me to shut that down with the quickness. Without warning, Rufus kicked me under the table so damn hard he almost flipped backwards, and that's how he played it off, by acting like he lost his balance. Timothy was about to jump over the table and choke Rufus's ass but couldn't because I was using his thigh as the source to take in all my pain by squeezing it. He took it like a trooper, and when he saw a tear slowly roll down my face, he wiped it away. Faith was oblivious to the things going on around her and kept right on talking a mile a minute. Once my pain subsided, daddy said "I told ya'll I would get it. The church picnic and you visited with my boys at church one Sunday." Rufus looked down at my father, put a big smile on his face and said "Yes sir, you're right on the money" as Faith asked "So wait, ya'll know each other?" As soon as she said that my phone vibrated. I looked down and saw a text from Jonathan that said "That niggas ass is grass!" I looked over at Timothy to see if he had somehow sneaked Jonathan in a text about Rufus kicking me, but when I looked over at him, he was looking down at my phone just as shocked as I was.

****

Timothy was just about back to his old self. He still had a little limp, but made that limp look sexy as hell when he walked. He wasn't going out like no punk and used it to his advantage. After the dinner incident and our merging back into college life, he let me know that my pulling away made him feel some kinda way, but instead of invading my circle, he gave me the space I felt I needed. I made no excuses for my behavior and instead of letting him in on why I had pulled back, I asked my friend to be patient with me and thanked him for giving me my space. I was still on a mission to pay Rufus back for hurting me, so I let that remain my little secret, and gave my friend a big hug. It seemed as if my wounds were just as raw that day as they were when the pain was initially inflicted. But the words that floated outta Timothy's mouth made Rufus's previous wounds feel like paper cuts.

Timothy took both of my hands into his and said "Joanna, I am begging you to leave that nigga alone. He is all the way live bad news. I can handle his fagot ass because of where I come from, but girl, you don't know shit about this nigga. He's dirty Joanna, and I'm surprised your brothers haven't dealt with him the way he needs to be dealt with." I was about to speak when he said "Shut the hell up Joanna! Damn! That nigga been selling videos of ya'll. That hotel shit been on the block for months. Hell, that nigga even got yo cousin on there, but her stupid ass was a willing participant. And the only reason Faith ain't on shit is because he said she's boring as hell and won't make him a dollar. I told yo ass that shit a few months ago but you didn't listen. You never listen!"

My mouth flew opened and tears started streaming down my face. The words that rolled off my friends tongue were more than I could handle. THAT! WAS! MORE! THAN! I! COULD! FUCKING! HANDLE! Daddy had always told us

"Don't play with sin, it'll take you places you never thought you'd go." Oh my God, what in the hell have I done!

I was so ashamed I turned my head away from Timothy. He took his index finger and lifted my head up towards him. I closed my eyes as I envisioned him watching me naked with Rufus. Timothy pulled me close, and in a soft voice he said "I didn't see the videos Joanna and neither have your brothers. But we do know about them." I put my face in my hands and wept, and although I couldn't confirm the things Timothy said as truth, I knew they were. The number one reason is because you cain't make that kinda shit up, but the number two reason is because it seemed as if no matter where I went on campus, I always heard somebody whisper "Juicy". I thought my mind had been playing tricks on me whenever I heard it because Rufus was the only one who called me by that name, but it wasn't. Those choir boys had seen the damn video. I wanted to go hide in the cave of a mountain and never come out. My bothers knew about, not the video, but the videos? HOW! FUCKING! HUMILIATING!

I was so disappointed with myself I couldn't put it into words. I was done. I was too through. I wasn't trying to pray, I wasn't trying to figure out how God was going to get me out of the mess I'd gotten myself into. And my parents, oh my blessed Jesus, what if they found out! Naw, I wasn't trying to do nothing on the spiritual, but what I did do was call my brothers.

They were at my house the following day, and when I opened that door to let them in I was so embarrassed, all I could do was drop my head. They sat on the couch while I sat in a chair, saying nothing. After a few minutes Jude said "Ladybug, hold ya head up." It took me a minute but when I did I noticed that Jude had his arm in a sling while Jonathan's face looked as if it had never been cut, which made me conclude that he was covering it up with makeup since Jesus ain't walking the earth healing folk like he did in bible times because that's the only way that deep scar could have vanished. He then said "We all fall short Sis. We all do, but we tried to tell you to back up off Rufus, and you didn't listen. Now half of Nap dun seen what you working with because of him. I don't know why you feel the need to be up around that boy, but do you see where it got you?" I didn't say nothin', just listened. He continued by saying "Joanna, my beautiful sweet Joanna. Why do you have to learn everything the hard way? Jonathan and I have known how this cat got down for years. His whole family is gutter. Do you think he chose you for nothing?" Jonathan quickly said "Shut it down Jude" which pissed Jude off. He looked at Jonathan like he was crazy, then in a soft calm voice said "Naw man, I think she should know". Jonathan stood up and said "Look Ladybug, we love you to death, and that's real talk. Something we don't have to tell you, but what I will say is this, if you keep fucking with that nigga, this will be my last visit" and then walked out the door.

I was shocked beyond being shocked. I looked at Jude like *what the hell?* He stood up too, and then grabbed me by the hand. He pulled me close and said "You are breaking my heart Joanna, but I have faith that The Lord will see you through this. I love you more than you'll ever know, but Bug, you dealing with the devil. Jonathan's in an all-out war with him and he's using you as a pawn which is why Jonathan's buying his time. But Rufus's days are numbered, and it's not because of anything Jonathan has told me that allows me to draw that conclusion, but the way he's living his life. He's a deceiver Joanna, and whatever game you playing trying to get back at him ain't gonna work, so you need to blow that candle out". *How the hell he know what I'm doing?* "The Lord has told us that vengeance is His Ladybug, and He don't need no help from you when dealing with the devil". As tears began to run down my face, I hurriedly asked "Then why are you fighting with him Jude? If vengeance is The Lords, why won't you and Jonathan let Him deal with Rufus?" Jude kissed me on my forehead and walked to the door, with his hand on the knob he turned and said "Jonathan is Jonathan, but I'm a work in progress Joanna and God is still working on me. Don't get me wrong, I'm talking to The Lord daily about what's going on, but it's almost like this invisible pull ladybug. You've got this invisible pull on my heartstrings keeps me..." Jude let that incomplete sentence hang in the air and opened the door. He blew me a kiss, then quietly whispered "All of the movies are off the street, every last one of them" and then walked out.

****

I don't know why, but I felt so defeated, lost and hopeless. I sat in the chair and didn't move for hours just thinking about my fucked up life. All kinds of niggas had seen my pussy and I felt fucked! My brothers were trying to protect me from myself and I had just shamed them to no end. I knew my Aunt and cousins had seen the video and probably watched it a thousand times laughing at my stupid ass. If my parents got wind of what was going on it would literally kill them both. I know people in all my uncles and even my dad's congregation knows about and or has seen the video, which was just as fucked up.

I had been playing Russia roulette and all the chambers had bullets. I started rocking back in forth in the chair. I felt like I was about to go fucking insane. I put my fingers in my hair and started scratching my scalp. I scratched and scratched until I felt a drop of blood fall from my nose. *What the fuck Jude mean I was being used? For what the fuck for? And what the fuck he mean they been going at it for years? What the fuck that mean? And what the hell they going at it about? These niggas on this campus dun seen my shit. They asses sitting up there whispering "Juicy" and shit like some weak ass pussies with they no dick havin asses. How in the hell am I supposed to walk around campus with that shit hanging over my head? FUCK IT, JUST FUCK IT!*

My self-esteem was out the window. I had allowed Rufus to take me lower than low, and I just didn't give a damn. It was almost like I let the forces that be take over my mind, body, and soul. I didn't even ask myself why. My mind was shaded with darkness with no self-worth left in it. My best friend in the whole wide world knew about the tapes and had lied about seeing them.

I would later learn that while Timothy was hanging at a frat brother's house, the guy had put the movie of me and Rufus in and once Timothy saw the content he told him to turn it off. The guy refused so Timothy started to bounce, and although the initial scene wasn't me, as he was putting on his jacket to leave the guy said "Daaaayum!" and that's when he saw that I was on the video. He asked the guy once again to turn it off, and when he flat out refused, Timothy kicked his ass, snatched out the video and then destroyed it. All that extra shit didn't even matter, just the fact that he got wind of it blew my skirt up. All the confidence and power I once had, was nonexistent. In my mind, when people looked at me all they'd see was a dummy, a whore, a tramp, a loser, a spoiled brat who took all her gifts from God for granted, a hard head, an unforgivable sinner.

Chapter Eleven

~Rufus~

Yesssss, come to daddy Juicccccccy!

Two days later I called Rufus and I was not the same girl he'd seen at the restaurant. Yeah, I looked the same, but now our spirits were alike. I told him "Get a room" and then hung up. He text me back a couple of hours later, *meet me at the auditorium in 10 minutes.*

As I was making my way there, Rufus drove past me with Faith in the car. Her dumb ass yelled "Heeey Joanna" while waving with a big smile on her face. I didn't even wave back. I saw some of the campus boys and I knew they wanted to taunt me because of the video, but Timothy shut that shit down, so instead they looked at me out the corner of their lustful eyes.

Rufus pulled up and I got in. When I looked at him he still had a red lipstick mark on his cheek from where Faith had kissed him goodbye. *This nigga bold as hell.* Our car ride was in total silence as he drove me to one of the luxury hotels downtown with key in hand. How the hell he did that with dumbass in the car was a mystery to me but when dealing with Rufus, he played by his own rules so he did what the hell he wanted not expecting any consequences in return.

When we got to the hotel, Rufus walked around to my car door and opened it for me. He held me around my waist as we walked to our room. When I walked in, I didn't even look around to take in the beauty of my surroundings; instead, I took my clothes off and got into the bed. Rufus threw his car keys on the table along with the room key. He took his shirt off then stood there looking at me like *naw, this shits too easy, sumthins up.* After staring at me for a while he put his shirt back on, picked up his car keys and the room key. He then picked up my cloths, threw them at me and said "Put that shit back on" and then walked out the door.

Rufus drove me home, and again, it was in complete silence. He didn't even have his trashy music playing. When he pulled up to my front door I looked at him like *you ain't scared you gon get caught?* And in return he looked at me like *bitch please.* I got out and he drove away. I walked in and I could have sworn I saw Faith walking away from the window, especially when I saw the curtains moving, but when she ran up in my face telling me about her recent "Rufus adventure" I pushed those thoughts to the side and busted her bubble as she followed me with her high pitch ass voice and I slammed my bedroom door right in her face.

Two weeks later, as I tossed and turned while trying to fall asleep, I heard my bedroom door open and felt Rufus moving my blankets out the way as he started from my feet and kissed his way up to my lips. I wrapped my arms around him like he was my savior and deepened the kiss. I took in a deep sniff, and his ass smelled good as hell. He said "I've missed you Juicy". I just moaned and opened my legs in response.

Rufus licked my neck and slid his fingers down my pajama pants. I politely removed his claws and whispered "Naw nigga, I want the real thang". Rufus chuckled and said "You get what the fuck I give you" then sucked on one of my breast real hard. Out of reflex I slapped the shit outta his yellow ass. Rufus sat up on his knees, and although it was pitch black in my room, I know he was looking down on me. He sat like that for five minutes. It was like he was going through his rolodex of evil trying to figure out which one he was going to use on me. I don't know why but I wasn't even afraid. It was like I welcomed anything he had for me because I really didn't give a fuck.

Rufus unzipped his pants and opened a condom. He slid it on and gently pulled down my pajama pants and panties. He bent down between my legs and sniffed, then said "Damn Juicy yo shit smell good. I could sit with my face between yo thighs all day" and then teased me with one lick. He opened

127

me wide as he slowly put his log into my fire. That shit hurt hella bad but instead of running from the pain I welcomed it. Rufus ass started singing "Awww shit, damn yo shit tight, shit!" I felt my tears roll down the side of my face but once I adjusted to his size, the tears stopped and it started feeling good. Rufus told me "Yeah Juicy, get wet for daddy. Damn!" He laid on top of me and kissed my neck. He kept his head close to my face which allowed me to feel the hot breath of his passion.

While going in and out Rufus licked my shoulder and said "You taste so sweet", which caused more of my juices to flow, and I gripped his back. While going in and out, he kissed my collarbone and said "Your skin is so soft", which caused more of my juices to flow, and I kissed his cheek. While going in and out, he softly caressed my breast and said "Your body is so fuckin sexy", which caused more of my juices to flow, and I moaned. While going in and out he gripped my hips and in a hoarse voice said "I could fuck yo ass all day", which caused my juices to flow, and I started rolling my hips. While going in and out he sat up, grabbed my ankles, and opened me wide and grunted "Awww, fuck Joanna!" which caused me to grab my pillow, put it over my face and scream into it as my juices squirted out like a gentle stream. While still going in and out, Rufus squeezed my ankles, then deeply moaned, "Awww shit, oh fuck, awww shit!" fell on top of me, and let his own juices flow while moaning in my ear.

He lay on top of me breathing hard as both our heartbeats played a song for us. He kissed me on my shoulder, my neck, my face and my eyelids. He caressed my face and combed my wild hair back with his fingers. He got up and when he did, I leaned up on my elbows. As he was getting dressed, I saw a shadow move on the other side of the door, as if Faith had heard everything that went on and then tried to hurry up and leave before Rufus opened the door. Oh well! After getting himself together, he walked over to me and after finding my face in the dark, gave me a soft kiss on my lips. He walked to my door and said "I left you something" and then walked out of my room, and into Faith's.

I didn't even get up to see what Rufus had left me. I took my ass to sleep because I was still stacking my classes. Come morning, I had forgotten all about his "gift", until I reached over to turn off my alarm that was going off on my cell phone. Instead of my phone, my hand landed on a long box that felt velvety. With my eyes still closed, I put it on my chest and then found my annoying phone. I hit snooze, put my hand on the box, and then woke up fifteen minutes later when my alarm went off again. I was extremely tired but knew I had to get up. I leaned up to turn off my phone and that's when I heard the box drop. I sat up on the side of my bed, turned off my alarm, turned on my light, and then picked up my gift. I didn't have a lot of time so I rubbed the sleep out of my eyes with one hand, I opened my gift with the other and got the surprise of my life.

Inside was a necklace, bracelet and earring set, in the color of my birthstone, ruby. That set was so freaking beautiful and expensive, my damn hands started to shake, putting the other gift he'd gotten me to shame. I took one of the earrings out, held it up towards the light and then put it on. I walked to my dresser mirror and had to put my hand on my chest. That ruby red on my chocolate skin made that earring shine like a million bucks. I heard Faith's bedroom door close and that sound brought me back to reality. I looked at the rest of the jewelry lying on my bed through my mirror and didn't feel nothin'. Not mad, not jealous, not nothin', just void, like a shell. I said fuck it, took the earring off, put it back in its case, and then hid it in my closet, along with the ring he'd previously bought me.

Chapter Twelve

~Rufus~

You in the trap...

Rufus wanted to take me to a party off campus and when he asked, I readily agreed. The only other "parties" I had been too were with my church folk or family. Aunt B's parties were the best and a whole lot worldlier than other family members with alcohol and worldly music. Parties Jonathan and I made sure we never missed.

I was down for going to my first real party with Rufus, and besides, I'd made the dean's list again which made my parents proud, and kept them outta my business.

Rufus took me shopping and spent damn near 2000$ on my gear, making sure I out shined everybody who was going to be up in that piece. I didn't know what scavenger hunt he'd sent Faith on, but her butt had been ghost the whole day.

When Rufus picked me up later that night, he walked in lookin and smellin good as hell, with a little Louis Vuitton bag in tow. As he handed it to me he whispered "Here, put suma this shit right here on" while kissing me on my cheek. When I looked inside, I saw that it was another bottle of Shalimar perfume. I put a dab here and a dab there then turned around in a circle so he could see how good his coins looked spread across my flawless, youthful body. He got quiet, then got that *I wanna fuck yo ass bad look in his eyes* which caused me to laugh within. I rolled my own eyes up in my head, grabbed his hand and told him it was time to bounce because I wanted to get my party on.

When we got into the car, he had that ignorant ass underground rap music on, but I paid it no mind, I was on my way to my first real party and the anticipation had me on swoll.

The drive was about forty-five minutes, and when we finally got there, we drove up to a huge beautiful Victorian style mansion. I looked at Rufus with my mouth opened because the house was absolutely gorgeous. He looked over at me, gave a little smirk then pulled up to the valet. *What kinda party is this?* The all brick home gave Rufus's house a run for its money.

Rufus handed over the keys to his car then ran around it and opened my door. He took my hand, helped me out, and then slowly pulled me into his arms. He licked something off of his finger then gave me a deep kiss. My tongue started tingling so I yanked back from his grasp, then spit on the ground. I looked at Rufus *like what the hell?!* He didn't

132

respond, instead, he grabbed my hand and escorted me to the front door.

Rufus rang the bell and when the door opened, I saw the most beautiful white boy I'd ever seen in my life. He was tall and thin with wavy blonde hair that reached to his shoulders. His lips were perfectly shaped and oddly full for a white boy. But his eyes, they were so blue that when he looked at me it felt as if he was piercing deep down into my soul. He looked as if he should have been on a billboard or in a magazine somewhere he was so handsome. No introductions were made as Rufus and the guy embraced. Blue eyes stepped back as we walked in and that's when I noticed that Rufus acted very familiar and comfortable with his surroundings.

When the front door was shut, we walked throughout the house as Rufus made his rounds greeting people while holding my hand. Although everyone present were in their teens, they were acting hella grownup. They were all smoking, dancing and drinking like it was the natural thing to do.

Rufus asked me if I wanted something to drink and when I told him a 7up, he looked at me like I was slow and I looked at him like *right back at ju nigga!* He pulled me over to the bar and ordered two rum and cokes. I snatched my hand out of his then yelled "I said a 7up" over the loud music. He ignored me, handed me my drink and then grabbed my hand again, continuing to make his rounds.

The house was packed, and in every room we entered, Rufus was known. I saw a few chicks giving me the eye and I gave that shit right back. *Oh well!* If they wanted Rufus they could have him, I'd just wish them luck because his ass was a piece of work. I took a sip of my drink and to my surprise, it was quite tasty and didn't taste of alcohol like I had expected, so as he led the way, I sipped.

An old school slow jam came on which caused Rufus to stop and turn. That's the kinda party it was, one where people did what they wanted where they wanted. Rufus was looking at me as he downed his drink and placed his empty glass on a stair. While rolling his hips up against mine he said "Drink suma that shit Juicy so we can dance". I took a small, petite sip which caused Rufus to stop rolling his hips and start rolling his eyes up in his head. I started laughing which made him laugh. I took another sip, and then another.

Rufus was watching every move I made. I took so long drinking that drink that the song had gone off, but we didn't care because we were dancing with our eyes as we made our own music with nothingness. I teasingly said "I got one sip left, you want it?" He shook his head up and down. I gave him a little sly smile as I said "You gotta come and get it" then downed the last sip. Rufus took the glass out of my hand and put it too, on a stair. He then put his big hands on my wide hips and made sure I felt his hardness. We closed our eyes at the same time as he brought his lips to mine. I transferred that sip to

134

his mouth, and when some ran down my chin, he licked it right on up, then brought his lips back to mine. I wrapped my arms around his neck as he gripped my butt. I pulled him in so close I know his neck had to hurt. I broke the kiss then lazily took my hands and placed them around his throat and gently squeezed. Seductively, I let my hands slowly roam to his broad chest then wrapped my arms around his waist as the rum made me bold.

Rufus put his lips back on mine and slowly walked me backwards to the wall, then started gently rubbing on my body. I'd had my hands on his butt when I felt another hand squeeze his ass. I opened my eyes and saw a chick that had been staring Rufus and I down from the time we had stepped foot in the front door, walking away. I gave Rufus a little shove because that was a sure enough a buzz kill and besides that, the bitch was haughty as hell. Rufus was still in freak mode and leaned in for some more suga, oblivious to what had just happened, only to be greeted by my cheek. He stepped back a little perturbed, but that didn't faze me. Shit, I knew Rufus wasn't mine, but while with him I was going to be respected. I also knew how he got down when it came to females so I wasn't brand new to his moves. Hell, he had a baby by my damn cousin which was the ultimate level of disrespect, but I wasn't going to tolerate it that night. Once he realized the mood was gone, he kissed me on the cheek and we went and got another drink.

After a couple hours, *I was feeling real good.* Because I wasn't a drinker, the two I had consumed really had a hold on me. They had me feeling so good that when Summer Time by Will Smith came on, I pulled Rufus close and started to dance. He didn't budge. He just stood there with a crazy smile on his face as he watched me try to drop it like it was hot. *I was feeling real good.* I knew my ass couldn't dance, and that I was probably all the way lively off beat, but so what, I was having the time of my life. *I was feeling real good.* I turned my back to Rufus and started slowly rolling my ass up against his groin. I held up my arms as I shifted gears and started dancing to a song in my mind. I reached back and placed my hands on Rufus's head, pulling it down to the back of my neck, prompting him to kiss it. *I was feeling real good.* He took in a deep whiff of my perfume, then placed his hands on my hips and said "Damn yo ass smell good." *I was feeling real good.* I felt his worm grow into a snake as he pulled my hips closer. *I was feeling real good.* I laid my head back onto his shoulder as he licked and kissed my neck. *I was feeling real good.* I was erotically rolling, rolling, rolling my hips when I felt another pair of hands grip my waist from the front. *I was feeling real good.* And then I felt a kiss on the opposite side of where Rufus was kissing. *I was feeling real good.* And then I felt the gentle squeeze of my breast. Not too hard, not too soft, just right. *I was feeling real good.* It caused me to moan, moan, and moannn. *I was feeling real goood.*

The hands were replaced by a mouth. *I was feeling real good.* The mouth then kissed me all the way down to my "V". *I was feeling real good.* My hands left Rufus's face, and went down to the head that was bringing me pleasure. *I was feeling real good.* Rufus was pressing hard from the back, and the head from the front. *I was feeling real good.* Rufus's hands went under my shirt and oh so softly touched my breast. *I was feeling real good.* I lifted a leg over the shoulder. *I was feeling real good.* I heard a deep moan from down below. *I was feeling real good.* I started rolling my hips faster. *I was feeling real good.* As hard as I could, I pressed the head into my "V". Yes! Yes! Yes! *I was feeling real good.* They were about to take me there. *I was feeling real gooooood.* They were about to take me there. *I was feeling real gooooooood.* They were about to take me there. *I was feeling real good! Good! Good!* And right before I went there, *I WAS FEELING SOOO GOOD,* I lifted my head off Rufus's shoulder, *I WAS FEELING SOOO GOOD,* opened my eyes, *I WAS FEELING SOOO GOOD,* and looked down at the most beautiful white boy I'd ever seen in my life, *I WAS FEELING SOOO GOOD,* as his piercing blue eyes, *I WAS FEELING SOOO GOOD,* reached into my soul. *I WAS FEELING SOOO GOOOOOD!* And then they took me there, YESSSSSSSS!

****

Unbeknownst to me, I had just encountered my first experience with drugs. Well, I guess in actuality it was my second. The first was when Rufus had put that mystery substance on his tongue when he'd kissed me before going into the party. The second was when he'd slipped some of that same substance into my drink when we had gone for round two, and because I'd had my back turned, I was none the wiser.

Naturally, because I wasn't a drinker, I thought it was the alcohol that had caused me to let all my reasoning to be thrown out the window. But as I had laid in my bed thinking about what had transpired the night before, I knew there had to have been something placed into my drink, because I had never felt the way I'd felt the previous night, not even when I would sneak drinks at my Aunt B's parties. The strange thing is, I couldn't recall how I had even gotten into my bed, and better yet, I couldn't recall how I'd even gotten home, but what I could recall were pieces of a night that ended up being crazy as hell.

****

After the mini threesome, I opened my eyes and found myself in a room filled with a whole lotta people. The stench of sex was so potent, I covered my nose with my hand and thought *how in the hell did I get here? And where is Rufus?* My head was spinning so I closed my eyes again, and when I

138

opened them, I looked to my left and saw two girls kissing, *what the hell!* I closed my eyes, straightened my head and opened them again. My eyes connected with the deep blue sea. He bent down and kissed me, and I wrapped my arms around his neck and my legs around his waist, as he went in and out. When I opened my eyes again, the deep blue sea was gone, so I turned my head to the right, and that's when I saw Rufus with his hand wrapped around ass pinchers neck, as they argued. Her eyes met mine. *Did she just smile?* She turned her eyes back to Rufus's, then spit in his face. He hit her so hard, he knocked her out. As she dropped to the floor, he looked over his shoulder at me, and I saw the face of the devil.

I blinked and the devil was on top of me. He spread my legs wide and I welcomed him home. He moved soooo slow, or maybe the dope had me feeling that way. It didn't matter because I was in pure ecstasy. I felt hands all over my body and wondered *who's licking my fingers?* My head was floating as my whole body tingled. Somebody started sucking on my toes and a grunt from deep within escaped my lips. I felt a calloused hand caress my left breast as a small, soft, petite one caressed my right. I wanted to grab his butt and force him to fuck me harder but my captors didn't want to set me free, they loved my blackness. As I closed my eyes and listened as he whispered "Yesss, Joooooanna. Ohhhhh Joooooanna. I looooove yooooou." I opened my eyes as he said, "I abssssssolutely looooove yooooou." And then he stuck out his tongue, and that shit was forked.

Chapter Thirteen

~Rufus~

*You, my sweetnessss, are my addiction...you the
dope to my veinsss.*

In time, I couldn't tell who the devil was, me or
Rufus. It was like we had become one and it
happened so fast, I can't pinpoint when the change
began. I mean, it was like after that party, we
couldn't get enough of each other. Or better yet, he
couldn't get enough of me, and I couldn't get enough
of that euphoric feeling he gave me because if he
wanted some of my juicy juice, he had to lace that
dick with some powder. It would be during this time
in my life that it would be forever changed.

That first hit, that first taste, that first ingestion,
that first feeling, was oh so very sweet. I saw the
world differently. Life was to be lived, and it was to
be lived to the fullest, and I had found that door. The
sex, the sex, the sex was intensified. I wasn't just
riding the dick, I was riding the world. Rufus would
lick, and lick, and lick, *yessss*, his tongue was my

poison. He would suck my pearl, and when I'd lean up on my elbows, we'd look into each other's eyes, and they'd both be red as a setting sun over the horizon. He taught me how to lick him and he tasted sooo good. I held the power in my tongue, in my tongue, in my tongue and in time, mine became forked too. My breast were his mounds and as he'd lick them, his venom scorched them, but I loved, loved, loved the burn. His hands rattled, like the end of a snake. They rattled on my eye, my stomach, my mouth, my back. Whatever it touched, he'd use his venom to make it better and kiss it. He slithered his way into my pussy, my heart, my mind and I opened wide. The world we existed in was black with no light. I saw the good as evil and the evil as angelic.

I growled, WHAT THE FUCK YOU LOOKIN AT MAMA? *Slap!* Yes ma'am, Mrs. Amos, your pie is very good. WHERE THE FUCK DID DADDY HIDE THE 5,000$ WATCH JONATHAN GAVE HIM? Thank you sooo much Mr. Amos, I absolutely love the earrings! I hope you like the Christmas gift we got you. NO MAMA! I AINT GOING TO CHURCH! YEAH YOU DO THAT!!! HOW FAR YOU THINK YO PRAYERS GON GET?!?!? Ohhhh yes Mr. Amos, lick that pussy. WILL YOU STOP HAVING THOSE FUCKING CHURCH PEOPLE CALL ME! Rufus, I don't give a fuck about what you heard out in them streets because my brothers don't give a fuck about you or me! YOU DONT NEED TO KNOW WHERE I LIVE MAMA AND IF YOU KEEP CALLING MY PHONE IMA

GET MY DAMN NUMBER CHANGED! How many you want me to fuck tonight baby? I JUST NEED THE MONEY MOMMY, PLLLLEASE, I'M FUCKING SICK!!! Why we in this sleazy hotel Rufus? And why did your parents cut us off? WHY ARE YOU HAVING ME ARRESTED? HUH? I FUCKING LIVE HERE! IT'S NOT MY DAMN FAULT YALLS STUPID ASSES GOT THE LOCK CHANGED!!! What alley Rufus? And how many dicks ima hafta suck this tiiiime? I DONT NEED NONE OF YALL HYPOCRITES DOIN SHIT FOR ME! DO YOU HEAR ME DADDY? NOTHIN! Do I have too Rufus? I'm tired and hungry. SO WHAT? I GUESS IF IM DEAD IN A DUMPSTER SOMEWHERE, YALL BE HAPPY HUH? I'LL BE OUTTA YALLS HAIR FOREVER! Rufussss, I'm sick baby, I'm sick and cain't work tonight. Ooooouch, please stop, please! Ok, ok, baby, I'll go. I'll go. I NEED THE MONEY JONATHAN, DAMN!!! Rufus! Rufus! Rufus! Something just slid down my leg, and I'm bleedin'. DO NOT, NEVER, EVER CALL MY PHONE AGAIN! I cain't find a vein Rufus, here, help me tap~tap~tap. AUNT B DONT KNOW SHIT ANOUT ME! Slow down Rufus. Yeah, they at bible study. I'll be right back. THAT'S MY MOTHER FUCKIN MONEY! I WORKED AND SAVED THAT SHIT, NOT YOU! I know I'm skinny baby, but I'm still pretty. Don't you think I'm pretty? STOP FUCKING PRAYING FOR ME!!! IM TRYING TO FUCKING GET HIGH! Yesss, yesss, yesss baby. I DONT GIVE A

FUCK ABOUT WHAT PEOPLE ARE SAYING ABOUT ME! FUCK THEM!!! Can't you ask your parents, just this one time? I'm sick baby. WHO TOOK MY MOTHA FUCKIN CAR? HUH? THAT IS MY FUCKIN CAR!!! Ima suck ten dicks for your birthday baby. I want you to have the bomb high. STAY THE FUCK OUTTA MY BUSINESS, YA HEAR? STAY THE FUCK OUT!!!

~One year later~

"Mommy, I'm sick..."

She's there. They're there. Everybody except Jude. I'm admitted. I'm sick. So so so sick! I want to die! I feel like I'm about to die! *Mooooommy! Please help me mommy, please. OH MY GOD! I'm hurting.* It feels like my insides are being rearranged and it hurts. It hurts so bad! I'm in a ball on the floor. I'm rolling and rolling and rolling, back and forth. *It huuuuuurts!!!* My stomach, back and ribs hurt because I've been throwing up. It hurts to breathe. *Please, no food. Please don't make me eat that.* They feed me with a spoon, like I'm 6 months old, and I throw up.

After three months I'm able to have phone calls. When I hear my daddy's voice, we both burst out into tears. He can't talk and gives the phone to mommy with the same results. The only words that were spoken were when we said "I love you" before hanging up.

After another three months, they visit. I run into their arms and we embrace. I'm back, I'm Joanna again. I'm not that skeleton they picked up from the filthy hotel. I have a sparkle in my eye and I'm happy. We all cry, but when I see Jonathan, when I laid eyes on my handsome big brother, I fell to my knees. He was too macho to cry, but he did drop to his knees and hug me as I did.

Three months later I was home. I was healthy, and I was home.

Chapter Fourteen

~Rufus~

Yoooou belooooong to meeeee...

He slithered his way back in. He slithered his way back in!

I was home and happy, but different. I clung on to my mother, going everywhere she went. Initially she'd taken FMLA to be there for me during my treatment, but after I was discharged, she retired. She said she had to be home to take care of her baby, and that no amount of money was worth time away from me.

I lived and breathe the church. Whatever ministry my mama was in, I was in. Whenever her and my dad went to minister to a family or friend, I was right there with them, even if I had to sit in the car and wait. I didn't care; I just wanted to be around my parents. I started helping with the kids at church and formed a chorus group, and their parents beamed with joy at their first performance.

Jude was still ghost, but not my Jonathan. He never lectured me about my choices, and he would come over at least once a week, just to chill with me, watch movies, play board games or help me come up with songs for the kids. I was glad he showed mercy and never asked about what went down; I'm a hundred percent positive that he already knew.

Timothy called me from time to time, and although he wanted to be there for me just as I was there for him, I'd shut that door. I still loved him like a brother, I just wasn't ready for him yet, I just wasn't. He was on those verses of the day though, and never missed sending me one.

It was real strange, after I left school, Faith was ghost too. No matter how hard I tried to find her, she wasn't available. Her phone number was changed and when I asked a couple of people from school about her, there were at a loss just as I was, so I decided to just keep her lifted up in prayer and left well enough alone.

For the first few months, I was my parent's shadow, but eventually I started fellowshipping with the friends I had before I left for college. All the drama at school had happened within two years so when I came home, all my friends were 18 and about to leave for school. *I wonder if my parents regretted sending me to school at such a young age?* I hope they didn't because my age had nothing to do with what went down, it was my choice to listen to the voice of another that had caused my life to spiral out of control.

My church friends all looked the same, young and innocent. I know that when they looked at me they saw that my innocence was gone but they welcomed me with open arms.

One of my sisters in Christ asked if I would go to a gospel skate night with her. At first I said "Heck naw!" then immediately apologized. She didn't know nothing about me, Rufus and the rink, and I'm glad she didn't. After she kept begging me, I relented and said I'd go. I had a whole lotta anxiety about making that decision, but I was tired of living in a cage and besides all that, I missed getting my roll on.

My parents had taken my car and sold it so she had to pick me up. As we made our way there she was going on and on about a guy she really liked who attended one of my uncle's congregations. I listened but didn't listen at the same time. My mind was on the skating rink and who might be there. During the whole ride I prayed that Rufus wouldn't show up because I knew I would be stuck there since I hadn't driven, and knew I couldn't tolerate being tortured by his presence.

When we pulled up, I felt like I was walking through time and immediately regretted coming. As I walked in and paid, my mind took me to a visual of Rufus on the skate floor, to him looking at me, his hands going down my pants and my flushing his number down the toilet. It was too much for me to

148

handle, way too much. I called out my friends name and when she turned to look at me she asked "Joanna, are you alright?" and then I threw up. That incident let me know I needed to keep my black ass at the crib.

I soon learned that when dealing with Satan, you ain't got to go nowhere, because his ass will come to you.

****

With all the credits I'd received in high school, and the ones I got while in college, I was able to receive my associate's degree. Mommy and daddy were so happy we all went out to celebrate, even Jonathan. Of course, Jude was invited but didn't come.

We went to an authentic Mexican restaurant and threw down. When we got home I was so full I went straight to my bedroom. I didn't go to sleep; I just laid there flicking through channels. I came across a Three's Company episode I'd never seen and got comfortable. It must have been a marathon because two hours later I was laughing at something Jack had said when I heard my mom knocking at my door while announcing herself and walking in. With a humongous smile on her face she said "Your cousin Tamar came down to see you, and she brought my precious great nephew with her. I'm going to be out here with your Aunt B and the baby while you two catch up" then stepped aside. In walks my cousin and I'll be dammed if her ass wasn't pregnant again.

She walked in with her hand on her back like she was 19 months pregnant, when in actuality she was barely three months. She sat down like she was 19 months too, spreading her legs out while leaning back real slow as she made her way into my computer desk chair. I couldn't believe my ears when I heard her let out a long deep sigh as if the action of sitting down had taken all of the wind out of her. I rolled my eyes up in my head and turned my TV volume all the way up as she opened her mouth to speak. I wasn't trying to hear nothing she had to say, nor was I trying to talk to her. I guess her phone had been ringing because a few minutes later, out of my peripheral, I saw her hop up so fast outta my chair that if you didn't know any better youda thought it was a miracle. As she walked towards my bed, I saw her motioning for me to turn my TV down so that she could answer. I gave her a dirty look then turned that shit down one bar. I then looked at her like *that's all you getting bitch!* She rolled her eyes and started yelling into her phone, but didn't move. I got the feeling that she wanted me to hear her whole conversation. I ain't gon lie, my ears were bleeding to see if it was Rufus, and low and behold, it was.

While she was yelling I hit mute then looked at her with a smirk on my face like proceed. She cleared her throat and said "Now what you say baby?" I wanted to rip her throat out. She continued by saying "I thought you said yo mama was gon get the bassinet. Awwww baby. Ok". I wanted to spit in her face. She then said "Alright, I love you boo. Huh? I told you that my mama and RJ were going down the street. Ummm, yeah! She does live here!" I guess Rufus was doing some talking and he wasn't saying what she wanted to hear because she yelled "What the fuck you mean put her on the phone. Nigga, you got me fucked up!" then hung up. I just laid there looking at her with an eyebrow raised and a sly smile on my face, and then hit unmute.

****

Two months later my mom and dad were running around the house like chickens with their heads cut off. They said they had to hurry to the hospital because Tamar had been beaten dame near beyond recognition and they didn't know if her or her unborn child were going to make it. *Did I just hear what I thought I heard?* Yeah, my cousin was a straight up bitch, but she was still my cousin. We grew up together, played together, lied and cheated together so I joined the party and started looking like my parents as I tried to find my shoes.

This reminds me of the incident with Timothy!

When we walked into the hospital waiting room, half of the family was already there. My cousins and Aunt B were hysterical. Kids were running around all over the place like they had been caged animals and then I saw the kid Aunt B was holding, RJ.

When he looked up at me, I rolled my eyes then went and sat next to Jonathan. I couldn't help it. I knew deep down it wasn't that baby's fault but every time I looked at him I saw Rufus.

Jude was on the other side of Jonathan and acted like he hadn't even seen me. That shit broke my heart. I missed my brother! While growing up, Jude and I were closer than me and Jonathan, and with that being the case, I knew that if he wanted, he would be ok with never saying another word to me again.

I got up and sat on Jonathan's lap. Yeah I was too big but I was also a big baby. I wrapped my arms around his neck, and as I did I purposely let my hand rub up against Jude's shoulder. That pissed him off. With the quickness he got up and went and sat on the opposite side of the waiting area. I didn't care, I'd gotten what I wanted, and that was to touch my big brother.

After Jude had gotten up, Jonathan started rubbing my back in understanding, letting me know that he felt my pain. He tapped me on my leg and said "Come on Bug; let's go get some fresh air". I climbed off his lap and we made our exit. As we did, something told me to look at Aunt B. I slowly turned my eyes in her direction and saw that RJ was asleep in her arms, and that she was wide awake, following me with venom in her eyes.

We stayed outside for about 30 minutes. Long enough for Jonathan to smoke a couple cigarettes and long enough for the summer breeze to blow some of the cigarette scent away. I ask him to help me with a singing key in a song that I was having trouble reaching and wanted to make sure I had the right tone before I went before the kids and taught them something wrong. We were both leaning up against the brick wall of the hospital going back and forth with the pitch when an all-black Mercedes with tinted windows slowly drove by. Since it was dark out, there was no way we could see inside. The back window was cracked a little bit and I saw a pair of eyes looking right at me. Out of my peripheral I saw Jonathan do the same thing he'd done the day I was leaving to go to college. On the sly, he curled his fingers into the shape of a gun then pulled the trigger. Of course, like the first time, he didn't think anybody had noticed, but I had.

We went back inside and started to once again play the waiting game. I guess some other family members had come in through another entrance because our seats were taken and the place was beyond packed. That's when Jonathan suggested that we go to the cafeteria. Although they were closed, they had different options in their vending machines than the waiting area did. We found a booth and while eating snacks, we started making beats with our mouths while tapping on the table. I don't know how long we did that but I do know that before I knew it Jonathan was shaking me awake.

I stood up, yawned and stretched then put the jacket he had covered me with around my shoulders because I was freezing. I wondered *why do hospitals hafta be so dang on cold.* I looked up at Jonathan because he wasn't saying anything, just standing there looking down at me, and that's when I saw his red eyes. I whispered *"What"* while a lone tear slid down my face. I said "Jonathan, don't tell me Jonathan". He started blinking his eyes real fast and said "They gone bug, they gon". With my eyes on him I said "No, no, no, no, no, no, no please no" then ran into his arms. I was holding on to him tight, while still saying no. *Did he just say my cousin was gone? Not my Tamar?* A couple of minutes later, I felt another pair of arms embrace us. I didn't have to look up, I knew it was my Jude, and although he wouldn't talk to me, his touch said enough.

Jonathan said that he would take me up to see Tamar but warned me of what was to come. I told him that I thought I could handle it so he escorted me up.

When I walked in Aunt B was at Tamar's bedside looking down on her so I didn't immediately see my cousin, but when I walked up to her bed, I froze. I asked myself *Who in the hell is that person lying in that bed?* Because it sho ain't my cousin. I guess Aunt B heard me gasp because she turned around and said "This is all yo muthafuckun fault!" I looked at her confused *HUH?* I turned around thinking she was talking to somebody else but wasn't nobody in there but me, her, and Jonathan. As soon as she said that big bro said "Shut that down Aunt B." Aunt B turned to Jonathan, squinted her eyes and yelled "Nephew, what the fuck you mean shut that down?

My baby and grand-baby are dead because of yo selfish ass sister. Do you hear me! Dead!" then broke down in tears. Jonathan ran over to Aunt B and hugged her as she wept, in my mind I was thinking *her ass is crazy because I didn't have shit to do with this!*

I drowned Aunt B out and I looked at my cousin. I could not believe my eyes. Her whole face was swollen and it looked like one of her eyeballs was out because it was sunk into the socket. Her mouth was opened and I could see that half her teeth were missing. I felt like I was going to be sick so I averted my eyes. When I did they landed on her stomach which was still kinda poofed out. I don't know why but I walked up to her bed and stood where Aunt B had been standing and placed my hand on her stomach. It felt like a rock. I had subconsciously placed my hand on mine at the same time which was weird.

Out of the blue Aunt B grabbed me from behind by my neck and threw me on the floor while yelling "Don't you dare touch my baby! Do you hear me? Don't touch my fucking child!" She was in a zone as she sat on top of me hitting me with her fist. All the while she was screaming "He killed her because of you, you dope fiend bitch. You fucking bitch! Because he loves you!" I was shielding my face from her blows, still not knowing what she was talking about, but when she hit me in my damn eye, I started fucking her old ass up!

She had caught me off guard because Jonathan had gone out into the hallway to take a call so she used that as the perfect opportunity to attack. By the time Jonathan had gotten back into the room I was on top of Aunt B choking her ass yelling "What the fuck you talkin about? She was my damn cousin! She was my damn cousin!" Jonathan yanked me off of her like I was a broomstick and swung me around. Aunt B had the nerve to try to come at me again, and when she did, I tried my best to get out of Jonathan's arms for round two. I was crying, Aunt B was crying and Jonathan was yelling. When Jonathan put me down, Aunt B wailed "Joanna baby, come here baby, come here Joanna". When I walked into my Aunt's arms, she held me so tight that even a tsunami couldn't tear us apart.

The next day, everybody went down to Aunt B's house except me. I was too drained. And although I couldn't move my body if somebody paid me, my mind was in constant motion. My Aunt's words kept going through my head. *What did she mean he killed her because of me? And what was that craziness bout Rufus still loving me.* I wanted my brain to be still and not function but it wasn't having that. There were too many unknowns and it wouldn't rest until they became knowns. It was too much. Everything that happened was just too freaking much to process.

****

I could not believe Tamar and her baby was gone. Who was going to take care of her other two? They was some bad ass kids so whoever took them on was asking for trouble. *Oh my goodness, my cousin is really gone forever.* I know we had our differences, and I cain't lie to myself, at one time I actually hated my cousin and my Aunt for how they had done me. In my eyes, that was some unforgivable, never going to talk to you again kinda shit, but I had gotten over it. I guess there was still some good within me and I wasn't as lost as I thought I was.

I had gone down a dark path that had led me into the bowels of hell and Rufus had led me there. Although I refuse to place all the blame on him, I will place most of it. He used my cousin and family as if playing a chess game and everybody realized it when it was too late. Well, Jonathan and Jude probably knew what was up, but we women didn't. I could not wrap my mind around the fact that my cousin was gone because of him. I wondered if he did it himself or if he had somebody else do it. I knew the answer to that as soon as it popped into my mind.

Rufus was a bragger and he cain't brag about shit he ain't done. *I hate myself! I hate myself, I hate myself, I hate myself!* Because although I know that bastard killed my cousin, I fucking still loved him!

****

Mommy came in later that night and told me that Aunt B wasn't going to have any services for my cousin or her baby. She said that all of the in-laws had said that they would come together to make sure she was put away very nicely, but that my Aunt wasn't having it. She told them that Aunt B said that she didn't have any say when it came to burying her husband but couldn't nobody say shit about how she was going to do her child and grandchild. Three days later my cousin and her dead baby were cremated.

Aunt B had sworn she would never step foot in another church, and that's exactly what she meant.

****

About a month after my cousin died, rumor had it that Rufus was in the hospital on life support. *That's what the fuck he get!*

Three months later, while helping daddy and members of the church paint the church building, I got a text that said *I didn't have shit to do with yo cousin and her baby. That was some other nigga she was fucking around with.* I immediately got my number changed.

Aunt B would call me yelling and screaming. I told Jonathan. He stopped that.

I started having trouble sleeping. Every time I closed my eyes, I saw my cousin's sunken eyeball. Mommy took me to the doctors. We didn't want anything to trigger a relapse.

While at chorus rehearsal with the kids, I received a text that read *I've missed you Juicy,* so I got my number changed, again.

Aunt B started coming down to the house with RJ. She came everyday but Sunday, so she didn't have to risk being asked to go to church. Jonathan stopped that too.

I would sit out on the front porch every day and read my bible, and everyday a car would slowly drive past our house, and park down at Aunt B's. I stopped sitting on the porch.

Out of the blue Faith sent me a text. *How did she get my number?* I hit delete.

One day I was in the grocery store with mommy, and although I was listening to Christian music on my iPod, I had it low enough to hold a conversation. While walking down the bread aisle I could have sworn I heard somebody whisper "Juicy", but when I turned around, no one was there.

After worshiping one Sunday, I went into my room to change into something more comfortable and when I walked in I noticed that my bedroom window was slightly opened. *Wow, that's weird.*

That night I took my prescribed sleep aid medication, and after a couple of hours, I was feeling real good and I saw the world differently.

Life was to be lived, and it was to be lived to the fullest, and Rufus had reopened that door for me...

THE END

Angela Moore

Conversion of A Pimp: New Beginnings and Sad Endings

~*Sophia*~

We met soon after I'd gotten pregnant with Jacob. Initially I would say that luck had brought us together. While reasoning with her about that truth, she'd look at me with her big pretty brown eyes, cut me off and come back with "Baby, there's no such thing as luck. This is my Father showing His loving mercy towards me". As time went by, and our relationship grew, I would learn that her getting God's mercy was an understatement.

****\

When I got the news that I was going to be a mommy, I was so happy; I could barely contain my joy. I still didn't have any friends, so the only people I could celebrate with were other hoes, and I selected who they were. I hadn't forgotten about Phoebe and her sheisty behind. Besides, I had heard about Joseph forcing other girls he'd gotten pregnant to have abortions, and the ones that defied

161

that order had their baby beat and kicked out of them with his Steele toed boots.

I wasn't trying to have one of those envious hating hoes drag me into an alley and cut my baby out. Oh no, I kept my pregnancy a secret, and told only a select few. The girls I did tell were just as overjoyed as I was, until one , with a scared look on her face, asked "Sooo, when are you going to tell Joseph?" I had thought the same thing with the same fear. Little did I know, in time, I wouldn't have to tell Joseph, because he would end up telling me.

****

For some weird reason Joseph had taken me off the block and kept me for himself. He'd given me the assignment of being charge over the other girls along with some odds and ins to do on a day to day. My job, for the most part, was doing what some would call office work. Yeah I was fifteen, but I was a smart fifteen, so he used my brains to his advantage.

Now all of us girls knew that Joseph wasn't about wasting his time nor his money, so whenever he would check over the girls work schedules and realize I had some down time, he would use that available slot for himself and have sex with me.

During one of those sex sessions he said "Open them damn eyes Sophia", so I did, and for a split second I thought I saw love in his. As he was going in and out, he grabbed my hands. I squeezed them,

162

along with my eyes tight. With a hoarse voice he told me "Open them bitches up. I ain't gon tell yo ass no muthafuckun more". Although it was hard I opened them and kept them opened for as long as I could. To restrain myself I arched my back and squeezed his hands tighter. He bent down and sucked on my breast which hurt like hell because they were so tender. He took his tongue and rolled it around my nipple which caused me to close my eyes and moan. When I realized what I'd done I opened them up real quick. I was NOT trying to get knocked upside my dome. He placed both his elbows on either side of my head and started kissing and licking me on my neck. In a strained voice he asked "When were you going to tell me Sophia?"

He had been sexing me down so good that I had snuck and closed my eyes again because he wasn't looking. But when he asked me that I opened them wide not knowing what the hell he was talking about. Joseph didn't miss nothing, so when he asked that question, I started going over the books and schedules in my head trying to make sure all my t's were crossed and all my i's were dotted. As I did he told me "Don't think about shit but my dick going in and out of you because if yo shit get dry ima fuck you up." My damn heart skipped a beat when he said that because either way uh ass whoopin' was coming.

Since I couldn't think and because I didn't know the answer to his question, I got so scared that I pissed on myself. When Joseph felt my warm urine

163

flowing over his rock hard dick he hopped back and growled "What the fuck!?" The look on Joseph's face caused me to scoot back on the bed and fold myself into a ball while still peeing, waiting on the blows. When they didn't come I looked up at that mean monster wondering why.

Joseph pointed his long black finger at me, and through clenched teeth said "If yo stupid ass wasn't pregnant I would beat you down! Now get yo pissy ass up and clean this shit! And Sophia, don't you ever, as long as you live, try to keep shit from me again do you hear me?" I shook my head up and down real fast wondering how he knew I was pregnant.

While still on his knees he stared at me for a long time and then crawled off the bed, keeping his eyes on me. He got dressed and then turned around to make his exit, but before he did he told me "I know muthafuckun pregnant pussy when I feel it" and then got ghost.

Ten minutes later I heard him having sex with another hoe, but that didn't bother me none because I knew that Joseph didn't waste a damn thang, not even a hard dick. And to be honest, I was glad he'd placed his attention elsewhere because as I sat on that pissy bed, I cried my heart out thanking The Lord that Joseph hadn't yanked me by my hair, dragged me to the back of the house, and commence to stomp my baby outta me.

****

When I told Joseph that I needed to start seeing a doctor for my prenatal care, he looked up from his TV, and then at me like "on second thought!" and went back to flicking through channels. When I saw that look on his face my mind went into panic mode so I told him that I would hit the streets to find him more girls to make up the cost of my doctor visits and my not being able to work. He gave me a real bored look that said "well what the fuck you still standing there for?" I turned and walked out the door. Three days later I had Joseph three new butterflies.

With that out of the way I started looking for a doctor. Some of the girls I'd worked the streets with had had kids before coming into the profession, and a few while they were still tricking. They all had plenty of suggestions, and I appreciated their input, but I had other plans.

****

After my mom died my dad left nothing out when he spoke to me of her. One of the stories he would always tell was how mommy had insisted on having an all-natural, water birth. He spoke on how she wasn't no half stepper, and wouldn't settle for receiving any ole kind of services, and wanted nothing but the best for her first born child. He also said that due to her dang near unachievable standards, it had taken her a while to find what she'd been looking for.

Daddy would go on to tell me that when mommy finally found a midwife who would deliver her baby while at home, and in their bathtub, she had broken down and cried. He would end by saying "Those pregnancy hormones had her crying so much, that if I told her I had to leave her side to go use the bathroom, she'd burst out in tears", and then he'd get a long lost look on his face. Sometimes, when he'd be telling me those stories, he would look so sad that I would want him to stop talking, but at the same time, I hated the fact that I longed for those stories to never end.

Every time daddy told me that particular story I would vow to have my kids the same way my mama had had me, naturally.

****

As I began my search online, I came across a midwife that was highly recommended and who was located not too far from where Joseph and I lived. Since it would be either Joseph or one of his workers taking me to my doctors' appointments, I made sure my choice was as convenient as possible, especially for Joseph. I didn't want him to have any reason to have second guessed the decision he'd made in allowing me to keep my baby.

On the day of my first appointment I was super excited. Although I had longed for Joseph to

166

experience this new chapter of our life with me I dare not broach the subject. I already knew the answer would be no. So instead of driving me to my visit he chose one of the girls to be my chauffeur. I hadn't wanted my first appointment to be that way but decided that in spite of my circumstances I wasn't going to allow anyone steal my joy and happily bounced my fifteen year old pregnant butt into the car.

As we drove around looking for the location we began to go further and further out of the suburbs, and deeper and deeper into the ghetto. When we pulled up to the location the GPS system had led us to I was in total shock. There was no way the building I was staring at housed the elegant facility I had seen online. There had to have been a mistake.

When my girl saw the disappointment on my face and wanted to leave, I told her to hold her horses. I was so geeked about being seen that if the location was legit and not a mistake, I was going to go ahead and go to my first appointment but find another midwife later.

I got out of the car, walked up to the building and saw a sign that read " dam ministries and rehabilitation facility" on the front door. I opened it and walked in hoping that what I was looking for was somewhere within its walls. When I got to the front office, I saw a real pretty chocolate lady sitting behind a desk. I soon realized that other than her, the facility was probably empty. She stood up with her purse over her shoulder as if to leave. I guess she hadn't seen nor heard me walk in because when she looked up and saw me standing there, one of her hands flew over her heart, and the other in the air, like she was saying the pledge of allegiance. In that pose, and with her eyes closed, she said "OoohmyholyandrighteousblessedJesuswhodwellson high" so fast; I didn't understand a word she had said. After saying that mouth full, she exhaled long and hard. I guess she'd also said a prayer because after a couple of minutes of her standing like that, she said "Amen" and then opened her eyes.

I stood there looking at her like "what the hell!?" With a small smile on her face, she began apologizing; "I am so sorry but you scared the living dickens outta me chile. Lord have mercy! This ain't the best neighborhood to be getting caught off guard in. Now what can I do ya for?"

I noticed she had a really deep raspy voice, like she was a heavy smoker, and that she spoke as if she was educated. As she stood there with a simple smile on her face I rambled off my purpose for being there, and at the same time, took quick looks at my watch. I'd intentionally left the house an half hour earlier than what I'd needed too in hopes of making sure that nothing would hinder me from being on time to my very first prenatal appointment. But, as I stood there speaking with the lady, my gut told me that there would be no doctor's visit that day, which caused me to burst into tears.

The lady dropped her purse, and with a worried look on her face, ran from around her desk and lovingly embraced me. I started mumbling about how it was my first pregnancy and how I wanted everything to be perfect and how things were messed up before anything had begun and on and on I went. She led me to a chair and rocked me back and forth while listening. Then I told her "You should probably get a bell over your door so you won't be surprised when people walk in" which caused us both to start laughing. She huskily replied "I would if my cheap brother would put it in the budget" which caused us to laugh some more.

She got up and handed me the box of tissue that was on her desk. Realizing that my day had been wasted, I rose as well and began walking towards the door. As I was making my exit, I started profusely apologizing for breaking down in front of her while at the same time wiped the snot and tears off my sad face.

After I handed her the tissue box, she ran to her desk and pulled out a business card then asked "What's your name baby?" With my hand on the doorknob I turned around, sniffed and said "Sophia". She stood there, crossed her arms across her chest and sang "Reeeeeally now. Wisdom, did you know that that's what your name means in the bible"? I didn't know nothing bout no bible, but what I did know was that she had some wide ass hips. While walking towards me, she softly sang "Helloooo, earth to Sophia" in her deep raspy voice while snapping her fingers. I put my eyes back on her pretty chocolate face and as she laughed, she handed me her business card and walked me to the front door.

Before I stepped out she gently touched me on my shoulder, prompting me to turn and told me "Sophia, if you ever need to talk, don't hesitant to call me. You, my love, are a child having a child and before you get all "tude" up, know I'm not judging you. I too had a child at a young age." She stopped mid-sentence and closed her eyes and when she opened them they were misty. "I too had a child as a child. I made some bad, bad decisions Sophia, and if it wasn't for the grace of God I wouldn't be here today. I just want you to know that I've been there, and if I can help you or any other young girl for that matter by showing you guys a better way, I'm in it to win it." Her words sounded like the words of a mother, something I never had and I appreciated her for that. We embraced one more time and then I said "Thank you so much Ms..." I flipped her card around to look at her name because she'd never given it, but there was no need for me to do that because before I could read what was written, in that manly voice of hers, she said "Amos, my name is Joanna Amos".

My mouth dropped opened as I realized that I was talking to none other than "The Bitch" herself, Joseph's mother...

Angela Moore

About Angela Moore

Angela Moore

Angela Moore has worked as a respiratory therapist at the VA Hospital in Indianapolis for fourteen years. The biological mother of three (but mother to many) is a faithful member of her church and the grandmother of three. In her spare time, she enjoys roller-skating, swimming, and fellowshipping with friends and family, both near and far.

Angela Moore

Conversion of A Pimp Book Series:

Joseph
Joanna
Joanna II

Coming soon:

New Beginnings and Sad Endings
Family Ties
Judgment Day
Salvation Has Been Brought Down

Order books at www.booksbyangie.com.
Also available on Kindle and Amazon in
paperback.

Conversion of a Pimp: Joanna II

www.ingramcontent.com/pod-product-compliance
Lightning Source LLC
Chambersburg PA
CBHW071217260626
47162CB00004B/1326